The Mountain.

Ian King Hamilton was born in Dumfries in 1955. He lives in Buxton, Derbyshire with his wife Jeanette, occasionally Rick, Rob and James, their 3 adult children, Titch the dog and Maumau the cat. He speaks French, German and Spanish and also writes theatre reviews and short stories.

The Mountain

The Mountain

By Ian King Hamilton

The Mountain

Copyright © Ian King Hamilton 2012.

Ian Hamilton

Acknowledgements:
Cover illustration by Mister Hope
(Mister Hope.com)
Edited by Jeanette Hamilton.
My thanks to John Merrill for granting permission to refer
to the story Winnats Pass Murder quoted in his
bookLegends of Derbyshire and Derbyshire Folklore
(johnmerrillwalkguides.com)

Mister Hope

The Mountain

To Jeanette and to Curt

Who made me realise how much I needed to write this.

☐☐

Chapter 1

It's the rain that gets you here, it's always the rain. The cold rain lashes your face and whips your ankles, there's no respite and no escape. The rain is angry, spiteful, it hates the morning. The rain is grey. The job – any job – would be so much easier, so much more possible, without the rain. 8.30 on a gloomy September morning, when the wild autumnal wind is already beginning to bite and the leaves are already dying, rustling in protest as they are dragged along the gutters, through the cold streets, would seem so much more bearable without the rain. This rain will outlive you, will outlive me, it will outlive this town. The rain will never stop, it will never die.

Chapelton High Street is like any other small town high street in Britain (except with more rain). The buildings may once have been elegant but are now a tacky tawdry mess of shabby grey stone; everything is grey. They tell of years of continued disrepair, they are run-down and largely unoccupied. The shops have mostly shut down, only the ubiquitous charity shops can afford the rates. "Britain isn't working!" and "Thatcherism isn't working!" proclaim the hoardings from high up on the facades of the empty shops. These dismal grey shop facades bear witness that Chapelton High Street isn't working, either. They are the legacy of neglect, Thatcher's unwanted children, as are their dull-eyed, weary owners, sent upstairs to their rooms when their presence might embarrass a visitor.

The Mountain

Years ago this was a small mining town. The last pit was shut in 1984, after a year-long battle against Thatcher's private army. If you look carefully, you can still see the scars – the redundant pit heaps, the disfigured landscape, the rusting pit shafts and chimneys scattered about these forlorn hills. The rows of pit cottages, too, stand empty, their windows and doors boarded up. The men I pass huddle stooped to protect themselves from the rain, but it is an uneven battle; the grey women and the children are old before their time. I am new to this town but I have seen their expressions before. These joyless eyes are known to me, and they are resigned to the fact that there is no hope.

The school gates are green and rusty, their imposing height and sharp spikes suggest that this is not a place designed for easy escape. A gang of brutish looking youths flank the steps of the nearby leisure centre, smoking with an urgency that is at odds with their otherwise apathetic stance. Music blares from a radio, girls huddle around a boy-racer in his car, and two boys indifferently kick a football at each other. The inscription "Chapelton Community College – visitors please report to reception" is my official welcome to the place where, as from today, I shall be working.

I am nervous as I pick my way through throngs of adolescents, boys braying with laughter, girls studied in their lethargy. My palms sweat as I ring the bell at reception, my ears are hot and I can hear my own blood. "Nigel Charon," I announce to a heavily made-up middle-aged lady, who appears to be paying no attention. I am struck by how strange and, well, foreign my own name sounds when I say it.

"Ah, yes," she appears to say to her typewriter. "I'll tell Dr White you've arrived."

Dr White is the head of the school. He is tall, thin and unhealthy looking, his pallid features and mournful face silhouetted before the bay window in his office. His

7

face is curiously misshapen, as if a mild earthquake fault has caused the left and the right side to be mismatched, causing his left eye to be fractionally higher than the other and his watery smile to be twisted. His lugubrious countenance betrays no warmth as he shakes my hand.

"Welcome, Mr Charon," he intones, rather in the manner of a chief villain in a film. "We trust you'll be very... *happy* with us. I'll show you to the staffroom."

I feel uneasy at this prospect, yet relieved at the thought of no longer being in his company. We walk past still more gangs of youths – how many of them are there? – who exude a smell combining wet hair, chewing gum, fizzy drinks, sweat and tobacco. The building is dark and dusty and like a maliciously designed maze – I have no idea where we are.

"Ah, John," says Dr White to a self-important looking man in a black suit coming out of what proves to be the staffroom. "Nigel Charon. Perhaps I can hand him over to you. He's part of your team."

"Welcome," says John Gillespie, head of fifth year. "Pleased to meet you. You're going to be a fifth year tutor, the first part of this morning will be spent with your tutor group. Any questions?"

I wonder what I am doing here, but feel that this is not the best time to share this feeling, so I remain silent. "Then follow me."

The staffroom is, if not as daunting as the corridors full of ugly adolescents, nonetheless an intimidating place with a disagreeable atmosphere. I feel afraid; I have felt this fear before. There is too much bustle and business for this time in the morning, and I am not accustomed to it. A door opens, Dr White re-enters, and it falls as ominously silent as it was intimidatingly noisy a minute ago. All wait in anticipation. Dr White stands by the door and prepares to speak.

The Mountain

"Welcome to a new term, colleagues," he begins, with a lopsided grin that betrays no mirth, I feel, no humour, but some quality altogether more disquieting. He leers as his gaze circumnavigates the crowded room, his beady eyes like those of a demented bird of prey. Then my blood runs cold as I hear my full name pronounced for the second time this morning, and the effect is more disturbing than when I heard myself pronounce it.

"Mr Nigel Charon is the only probationer to join us this term. I know that you'll all join me in making him feel" – his eyes alight on me as he makes his TV villain's pause – "most welcome."

Dr White continues to talk at length about exam results and money, building projects and outside agencies, working groups and senior team meetings, governors and leases for this and for that. He is rarely interrupted. At no point do I hear anyone mention children. I understand very little of what is said and catch few of the allusions, yet it comes as a curious kind of relief to me; I am no longer the focus of attention and the anxiety I felt before soon melts into this river of bland tedium. Indeed the forty – five minutes of his pre-term address seem to pass quite quickly, not, as I am keenly aware, due to his inspiring oratory skills so much as to the fact that when he has finished I shall be in sole charge of a class of children here for the first time.

"Ah, Anthony," Dr White breezes in quite a different tone of voice than his speech – but it is only really now that I realise he has *finished* his speech. "Nigel Charon, your new charge. Perhaps I can…hand him over to you now?"

Of course I have met these people before, on the day of the interview and on another day, but it seems now these were mutual charm offensives – they were eager to impress me and persuade me that I wanted a job there, I was desperate for a job I thought I had little chance of. Everything I had tried so far had failed and to put it at its most banal, I needed the money badly. Today the shine has

definitely been removed, everyone has taken off their mask
and it is all more real. As I shake the rather sweaty hand of
my new head of department, Anthony Marshall, I try to
work out whether this is on balance a good or a bad thing.

"Nigel, welcome!!" he effuses. "Welcome. So
nice to see you again."

"Glad to be here," I reply, unconvincingly.

"So how are you? Good holiday? Fancy a brew?
There's so much to do, isn't there? Well, better
get this

show on the road!"

Anthony is about forty-five, short, fat, bald and a
bit sweaty. He is jolly, and is the only person I've met in
this whole town to emanate any human warmth. However,
something about him strikes me as a bit superficial. He
walks here and there in an important, bustling manner but
without actually accomplishing anything. He asks a lot of
questions but by the time I've thought the answer he's two
steps ahead of me. He doesn't always wait. He talks as he
walks and uses a lot of technical jargon I don't fully grasp.

"Period 4 today you kick off in anger, 5B2
German. They're a shower, I had most of them last year.
Mostly basic level, if they're lucky, ex set 3 and 4. Start
with personal information, group questioning, open-ended
questions, pairwork, maybe a small consolidation exercise
towards the end. It's a struggle to keep them going for
seventy minutes, particularly at the end of the day.
Strategies for motivating and useful differentiation will be
called upon."

During break the staffroom is if anything busier
than it was when I first saw it, what seems like days ago
but was only this morning. I'm struggling as it is to take
this surfeit of information in, when John Gillespie
interrupts us.

"So sorry, Anthony, I really need a quick word
with young Nigel here. Nigel, welcome again, your form is
5Chn. You'll spend period 2 today with them, registering,

most of the time getting them to fill in their timetables. Uniform letters, PTA letters, the routine admin can be left until later. They're a very mixed bunch." He breathes in deeply, puffs out his large chest and almost whispers to me: "Start as you mean to go on with this lot, my lad. First impressions count for everything in this game. I've been doing this job long enough to know. Distance is required at first. Don't tolerate any backchat at all. You make your mark today, and they'll respect you forever. On the other hand," he pauses dramatically, "I've seen some colleagues who started out by being useless, and twenty years later they're still useless. Lose them, and you'll never get them back. At the slightest sign of any misdemeanour, send them straight to my office, A21. You have my full support."

The last bit reassures me somewhat, as my form room is A7 so can't be far away. Even so, it is with heavy steps that I join the more senior Pavlovian dogs on hearing the strident pips which signify the end of break and the real beginning of my new adventure.

As I fight my way along the corridors, I realise how unprepared I am. Where will they be waiting? How do I seat them? What if they chew gum? I can't do this! Nervously, I ask a thickset, greasy-looking brute for directions to A7. Following my nose more than his inarticulate answer, I arrive late, to find only six or seven girls loitering aimlessly around the corridor in what could loosely be described as near the room.

"Morning," I say, more cheerfully than I feel. "I'm your form tutor, Mr Charon. This is a small group."

A large girl with streaked blonde hair and multiple earrings and love-bites gives me a withering look.

"Others have went in," she informs me.

"Others have *gone* in," I say, with what I hope is a friendly yet firm winning smile.

She stares at me blankly, but hers is perhaps the most receptive and attentive face of those present. I

11

hesitate; I am at a loss before even entering my first classroom, which isn't even to teach a proper lesson.

"Well," I falter. "Where do you usually wait? Do you line up outside? Do you go straight inside?"

Three or four more of the group approach me now, at quite close quarters. Bored of whatever game they were playing until now, perhaps, or possibility to have a closer glance at this latest curiosity. No-one answers. A piece of inspiration comes briefly in my direction.

"Well, what did your form tutor ask you to do last year?"

Apart from a fat girl who sniggers, no-one appears to have heard. After what seems like minutes, a third spokesperson emerges; perhaps now they are tired of toying with their quarry.

"Dunno," is the measured contribution of a very small underfed looking girl. "We were all in different forms, weren't we? They mixed us all up."

For reasons probably associated with my by now visible discomfort, this remark instigates more mirth amongst the group. In an attempt to be purposeful and decisive I open the door to find a large group of youths sitting on tables, chatting, playing cards and in two cases throwing a football. A fat girl sits alone at the front crying. It is an unusual introduction to our working together, and such a surprise to me that I am lost for words. I hesitate still further; do I send this group out, or herd the other one in? The outside group take the decision for me, pushing past me as I stand perplexed in the doorway.

I optimistically try to salvage something from this mess.

"Now all listen, please," I begin, but no-one reacts at all. "LISTEN!!" I shout. A couple of girls turn round sullenly, the footballs stop flying, but otherwise there is no obvious effect, indeed no sign to an outside observer that I am even in the room. Then the faintest of knocks is heard on the door. I turn around to open it and am confronted by

The Mountain

the be-suited figure of John Gillespie. I turn back and
notice that my new form are all sitting like young model
citizens behind their desks.

"Morning again, Mr Charon," he says icily. "How
are we all getting on? I said I'd be around with blank
timetables."

He hands me yet another pile of paper and turns to
make for the door, but wheels round again with surprising
agility. His eye catches a distracted looking girl with wild
tousled hair sitting in the front row. He stoops down at her
desk until his eyes meet hers, their noses almost touch, and
bellows: "Take that jacket off!!" This is one aspect of
classroom etiquette about which I shall no longer be vague,
although grateful is perhaps not the first word which
springs to mind. She must be able to smell his breath, he is
so close, she must be able to smell the coffee and biscuit
from this morning's break, although to her credit she
performs a creditable act of being completely non-plussed,
whilst nonetheless removing the offending jacket with
speed. I feel Gillespie is beginning to enjoy this, he is
getting into his stride, and something tells me this little
intercourse is not yet finished. It seems quite impossible,
but he moves his face even more closely to hers. He is
ready for the kill.

"Are you... *chewing?*" The dynamic range of this
stark question is stunning; the first two words are screamed
with the intensity of a demented football crowd, the second
one pitched a good tone and a half higher than the first,
then a pause, either for dramatic effect or because he has no
breath left, then that third, all important word is whispered
almost, with near silent incredulity, to such sinister effect
that I imagine for a minute that it has a double meaning:
defecating, perhaps, or worshipping Satan. He invites her
to open her mouth and inspects its inside with more
thoroughness than a dentist. The girl then moves with a
swiftness I would never have imagined her capable of,
towards the bin, I think she is going to be sick, but it is to

remove her chewing gum. A watery smile of satisfaction crosses the face of the predator. He makes for the door again, then checks himself and doubles back into the form room.

"Oh, and, do let me know how your new form are settling in, won't you, Mr Charon?"

The lump in my throat feels like a tennis ball, consequently I do not find an immediate answer; cold sweat is on my forehead and trickling down my back. To my surprise, my new form remain in their current mode, rather than their previous one for the remaining forty or so minutes. I call and fill in the register, give them their timetables and hand out a hundred boring letters, none of which meets any opposition or even comment. On hearing the bell at 11:55, however, their Pavlovian instincts kick in as well, as they knock over furniture and, at times, each other to be the first out of the door.

Over lunch I sit with Gillespie.

"Well, you seemed to have that lot fairly well under control," is his astonishing opening gambit. "A good thing, too, as they will remember their first impressions of you. Younger colleagues do not always realise this, but you'll see – the way they were with you this morning is the way they will be with you all year." I am not sure what to think about John Gillespie. He has bailed me out but he is the most pompous person I have met today. He sports five expensive looking ball-point pens lined up neatly in the breast-pocket of his suit. During the meal I am introduced to various colleagues, but names do not sink in and faces struggle to make an impact. How will I ever remember the names of all those damned children? Most colleagues are older than me and look like the kind of people I would normally cross the road to avoid. I notice one or two younger, more normal looking people amongst the diners, people whom I would probably just quite like not to speak to, instead. One or two even mention going to the pub at the end of the day, which for me cannot come soon enough.

14

The Mountain

After lunch I have a free lesson, which I can spend in quiet reflection, if such a thing is possible in any institution housing over a thousand lunatics. I wonder whether I have really made any impression on my form. They ignored me completely at first, yet after the pre-emptive intervention of Genghis Khan they settled down very well. How much have I got them under my control and how much are they playing with me? I will find out a little more about how I cope at 2:45.

Once again the time has passed very quickly, the one plus I can see about the job after my career total of three hours and fifteen minutes (excluding lunchtime). Anthony Marshall has whizzed in and out of the staffroom on numerous occasions throughout my free lesson to little or no visible effect. He has piled textbooks, excrcisc books and markbooks, along with more reams of paper into my arms but that has been it as far as his input is concerned. Already I am faintly irritated by the fact that our Monday afternoon free lessons coincide. He is full of "Hail, fellow, well met!" type of good cheer but I feel there is little substance. At 2:45 he says to me something like: "Up an' at 'em, kid!" as if I am a popular but over the hill ex-boxing champion about to start the 15th round against the much-fancied, winning-on-points young contender.

On this occasion, also in room A7, I ask the class to line up outside. I am quietly pleased with myself. They do so, come in quietly, and stand behind their desks until I utter the command: "Setzt Euch!" I am still quite pleased, they appear so shy that they dare not move, so I repeat the command: "Setzt Euch, bitte!" Still no reaction comes from them, although in a very different way from with my form this morning, I am still being ignored. After repeating my instruction, it dawns on me slowly that they are not simply being polite; they don't understand me. I try again several times, using all my acting and miming techniques

and facial expressions grimly remembered from my
idealistic teachers' training course, but to no avail. I may
as well be asking them the GNP of a small South American
country, or the atomic mass of uranium. A large girl sitting
very close to me at the front stares blankly, her large eyes
peering through a thick curtain of long black shaggy hair,
radiating good will but her dazed expression shows all the
comprehension of a cow looking through a fence.

"All right," I concede. "Sit down."

To break the ice, I call the register. It is still quiet,
and I wonder if I could fill a bit more of the lesson by
calling it again, perhaps half-way through, then again
towards the end. I brace myself and decide to be business-
like.

I stand, look around, smile and pick on a harmless looking
red-haired boy sitting near the front.

"Wie heisst du?" The effect is similar to my
inviting the class to sit down and the poor boy grows so red
I no longer see his freckles.

"Wie heisst du?" I repeat, calling once more upon
my winning smile. "*Ich* heisse Herr Charon. Wie heisst
du?" This has no effect, possibly because the only possible
cognate in my example, Charon, is a sound he has never
heard before. "*Your name,*" I whisper, and hate myself for
being so patronising; the boy looks as if he is going to cry.
"Just say 'ich heisse' and your name." There is a pause.

"Ich heisse Darren."

The relief I feel is immense. I have just won over
the hearts and minds of my first class, they will all respond
to this template, it will be plain sailing. Sure enough, some
others in the class begin to respond.

"Ich heisse Leeann."

"Ick hise Wayne."

"Ish habe Rachel."

"Eek his Fiona."

This is working according to plan, and the
interchange becomes more advanced as I grow bolder.

The Mountain

"Wo wohnst du? Wie alt bist du? *Ich heisse Herr Charon, ich wohne in Chapelton, ich bin sechsundzwanzig Jahre alt."* My example will be an inspiration to them all.

"Ik wonne in Chapelten, eek bin firzen."

"Ick wone Chapelten, ick hise firseen."

The dialogues continue thus for a while, and I am feeling very pleased, realising now why I opted for this profession. I am enrichening their lives and they are eager to learn. I look at my watch fleetingly; 3:00! We have another fifty-five minutes to go! A few more questions, because we're on a roll. I catch sight of a thin, sulky looking girl sitting in the front row who is yet to join the discussions. I move to in front of her desk.

"Und wie heisst du? Wo wohnst du? Wie alt bist du?" Three questions all at once is the most ambitious move in my career so far, but we can do it.

There is no response. I repeat the questions, together at first, then individually. The girl sits impassively, staring into space, her pale blue eyes seem lost and she lowers her face as if trying to hide it completely. This is taking time and the momentum of the lesson is being lost. I'll try just once more and if not -

"Sir, she don't talk."

The intervention is on the part of a large, jolly looking girl with blond curly hair and glasses.

"I beg your pardon?"

"She don't talk."

I sigh. "We none of us want to talk at first, when learning a foreign language, we're self-conscious, we don't want to sound silly, make a mistake, it's a very British thing, yet one of the most effective-"

A chair scrapes loudly and the large girl stands up. "Listen. She don't talk. It's not what she does."

There is a distinct background murmur in the room now; the long-held background silence has been broken. I gather my wits, but all I can come up with is:

17

The Mountain

"She *doesn't* talk." Suddenly everything descends into chaos. Hitherto silent boys in the back row bray like donkeys, girls cackle like geese. In scenes which remind me all too clearly of this morning, pupils get up and walk around at random, sit on tables, throw objects, but this time it is actually *during* my lesson. I stand like the captain on the deck of a sinking ship, but instead of "Women and children first!" I choose to shout "Ruhe! Setzt Euch!" and then "Be quiet! Sit down!" to no avail. Somewhere I can hear a Walkman. This is no longer going according to plan. Throughout all the chaos two studious looking boys in the back row sit reading their books. The sulky girl in the front row says nothing and has not even moved.

The door opens and Anthony Marshall enters; I am actually pleased to see him. He looks aghast, perplexed, but momentarily at a loss for what to do.

"What is the meaning of all this…" he begins, but there is no follow-up. He looks around in disgust, then picks an innocuous looking pupil who is hardly doing anything and shrieks: "You! Yes, you, Downing, come here now!"

A small miserable boy shivers visibly and approaches the great master.

"Have you taken leave of your senses? What on earth is going on?"

The boy looks mystified, with some justification as he has been one of the more inobtrusive rabble-rousers of the last five minutes.

"Nothing, sir, I, we…"

This sentence trails off for a reason. The door opens again and at it stands John Gillespie. The room falls silent.

The next twenty or so minutes of the lesson take place with Gillespie at the back of the classroom, not unlike a particularly menacing nightclub bouncer. Anthony Marshall has sloped off to find something to do. For the rest of the lesson my class are angels and cannot do enough

18

to cooperate with me. At 3.55, they even remain seated. As I am about to invite them to leave, Gillespie approaches me.

"A word, please, Mr Charon."

We skulk outside the door like naughty pupils preparing a trick.

"We simply cannot have this kind of thing. You will see this class twice weekly from now until the end of the academic year! If you want to survive you must make your mark on them, without fail. We'll have words on the subject tomorrow. Now I've arranged to keep them behind to, er, talk some sense into them. You'd better go."

"Don't let the little bastards grind you down," says Anthony when I see him outside in the stock-cupboard. He looks around for something else to say. "Well, what are your plans now? Time for a quick one? They'll be open now!" is his requiem for today. I don't know why people say that any longer, when they're all open all day now. As we leave the building I think I hear someone say "Non illigitamus carborundum".

Geoff Lennox, the PE teacher, David Stanton from English, and Lou Miles, Business Studies are already in the pub when Anthony brings me in and makes several introductions. More staff arrive, a group of noisy laughing young ladies join us at our table. One of them appears to be wearing a bedspread. The pub, intriguingly named "The Swan with Two Necks", is small and homely, with a friendly landlord and conveniently situated for school - from inside you can hear the yelps of the children as they torment and torture each other on their way home.

Geoff is agitated and talking about football. He greets me with: "This time next week!" I imagine some hidden threat, some parent, perhaps, who has arranged to lie in wait for me with a baseball bat; perhaps someone plans to lure me in here before an ambush, but I can discern nothing behind his patchy beard and beady little eyes. He sighs: "It's in Mostar." His voice carries resignation, almost stoicism, and I feel that I am supposed to think, well, that explains everything then. I must look as vacant and stubbornly stupid as 5B2 did at about 2.50 this afternoon, because David takes pity on me and explains what Geoff has so far been unable to do.

"His beloved Celtic", he informs me, are playing Partizan Belgrade in the first round of the Cup Winners' Cup. Away. They'll be knocked out first round, you'll see." His voice is refined and plummy and he has a way of sounding well-informed.

"2-1," counters Geoff, and all this might as well be in a foreign language to me, but I hope I look reasonably interested. "We'll get the all-important away goal, then stuff them at Parkhead, you wait."

Lou says nothing at all but sits down and looks mysterious. The young ladies sit and giggle. Anthony seems slightly ill-at-ease in this younger company. The beer makes me feel suddenly very tired, this day has lasted a week. I gaze into the coal fire in the corner and let the conversation swim over my head. It is easier that way.

Chapter 2

I run. That's what I do. I take off and run. Over the hills near our place, through the trees, up to the Cross. I run at night. It's spooky, it's *ghostly.* All those dark mangled shapes. I don't run to keep fit. I hate fit. I don't *jog.* I run to get away. I just run.

School started. It's OK. I'm past carin' now. Last year I hated it, couldn't have hated it more. This year, I just don't care. I'll go. If I get pissed off, I'll run. First did that two years ago. Just left a lesson, out the front doors and into the woods, and ran. Up to the Cross. When I came back, two days later, they're like: "Oh! It's good to see you safe! You know, you really could challenge some of that energy a little more productively. What about the athletics team? There's a club in town. The cross-country season is almost upon us." I'm like "I'll let you know if I want to be part of your scuffin' cross-country season which is almost upon us." That was when I talked to them; I don't now.

Teachers. They think they know, but they don't. They used to have a go at me, it's like "You talk back a little too much for your own good, young lady." Now it's like "You've got to talk to us. Open up. How can we help you if you don't talk to us?" Yeah *right.*

Got this new teacher. Bloke. German teacher and form tutor. Tried to get me to talk in German. Becky's like, "She don't talk," he goes, "She *doesn't* talk", she goes, "that's what *I* told you!" Whole place erupts. He turns red. He goes "Well we'll just have to see about that,"

some teacher thing like that, jabbers some German at me.
Everyone laughs. People go, "Sir, Becky were only trying
to help" which gets him really mad. Then the lads get
goin', howlin' an' chuckin' things like lads do. So old man
Marshall comes in – "Silence!" He can't control us,
couldn't even last year, this new bloke can't, all of a
sudden the doors opens, it's Gillespie, face completely red.
He goes, "Silence, you rabble. You lot, this is a disgrace!
All of you stay behind at 3:55!"

I scuffin' hate Gillespie, an' I know he hates me. I
hate anyone who calls me 'young lady', but I hate him
most. He picks on me an' Becky. He *did* pick on us, now
I'm OK, I can do what I want. Since I stopped talking to
them, I can do what I want. I'm OK, I've got a condition.
I've got a syndrome. I'm a 'self-elected mute' so there.
I'm special needs, so when I just sit and refuse to work, it's
OK. No-one dares have a go. It's OK for me, it's a bit
phoney, though.

I'm not goin' in today, I'm on a run. Up past the
Cross, the highest point of Chapelton. I got no education
but I know things like that. I know everything about these
woods. These are my hills. The soft, peaty bits near
Brown Moss, the limestone crags by Fenny Brook. You
don't get to know them in a school. I love the dark
gritstone best. I like to go back of the cross, past the two
reservoirs, up above the trees onto Pike Pass and sit on the
rocks. Takes hours. I sit there hours too. I watch the birds
in the morning. My mates would laugh, but I watch them.
I love the sound of the curlew. This is the only time I feel
real, out here.

We live near here. It sounds nice but it's not. We
live in a static caravan in a trailer park. No-one at school
knows exactly where. It's better like that. The council
would move us on if they could. I think they're
embarrassed about Coombs Moss Park. Nice name but the

The Mountain

place stinks. Me, Darren an' dad together in this skanky little caravan. It's freezin' and it stinks. I've got to look out for Darren a lot, takes some doing. I look after dad when he's fallin' over and that. And I look after myself. We eat, we huddle up to get warm, and we sleep. And that's it really.

I don't talk. That's not what I do. I *can* talk. I just don't talk to them. I haven't said a word to anyone (apart from Darren, dad, Becky and Tracey, maybe a few others) I haven't said a word since soon after The Smiths split up. I certainly haven't spoken to *them.* August 1987, they split up. After the beginning of third year at school, I sat at home and listened to the tape of *Strangeways, Here we Come*. I listened to nothing else. Just before Christmas, I stopped talking to them. All I did was listen to The Smiths, all year long.

Anyway today I'm on this run, it's a run I do every now and then. Up past the cross, past the reservoirs, Pike Pass and the rocks, and along this dirt track that I think only I know. It's the loneliest place in the world. I've never met anyone up here, and it's really high up. Sometimes I look back on the grey slate roofs of Chapelton below and think 'I'm glad I'm here, not there. The rocks are high on either side of me now, I can't see nothing except down this long, muddy path. I'm headin' uphill, it's steep, into the rain, then back round the far side of the reservoir towards the valley. I stumble on a rock, the noise frightens a grouse in the undergrowth who goes 'bocup' in alarm and flutters, then tries to fly away. He makes me laugh with his spasticated flight, almost at ground level. Nothing makes me laugh in town, or at home, where I just feel nothin'. Out here I can feel.

I sit out here sometimes. I come up here to be alone. I come up here in all weathers, in all seasons. I sit and watch the heather, the gorse. I like the silence. Some sheep bleat on a faraway hill, Black Brook gurgles below

23

me, and a curlew whirs through the air above me.
Sometimes I see lapwings. Most of all, I like the silence.

The rain smacks my face as I run down the steep
hill into the valley. The stream is already goin' mad
although I'm still high up. Forty minutes or so, I'll be back
in town. Meet Becky or Tracey after school. Go for a fag,
or do some glue. Not with Tracey, she's too straight. She
won't even skank things from shops with us. But she
won't dob. She's loyal. If I could, I'd stay out here all
day, but you got to eat. I've got Darren and Dad to see to.
I feel sadder as I get nearer town. Even the fields and trees
seem a bit less real. The air gets greyer. It's Ok, but
everything real dies a little.

It's the rain that gets you here, it's always the
scuffin' rain. It rains so it goes right through you. I like
bein' above the cloud, runnin' through the cloud, then you
get under the cloud and it was all just rain. You think the
cloud was cotton wool, or candifloss, but it wasn't. The
rain down here is just ordinary rain. Like tears. On the
tops I can dream. I even sing. But down here it dies a
little, and it's just rain.

It's OK though. I like to run. Comin' down is
like comin' down after glue. It makes you sad. But I'm
not sad I was up. An' I'll meet Becky at 4, in the precinct.
I'm wet, I'm sticky an' covered in mud. Not often I feel
this good.

I stop as I get near town. Walk now, so I fit in
with the other freaks who stay down here. Walk down to
High Street, into precinct. Becky's there, with Tracey. I
must be late. Tracey goes,

"Ey up! Look what t'cats dragged in!" Becky's
got some fags. I think, these are the only two people I've
ever been glad to see.

Becky goes, "Where *you* been? Skiver!"

"Yeah!" goes Tracey. "School were right mank.
We missed you."

The Mountain

I goes, "Never mind that. Did anyone notice?" Like I care.

"Did they 'eck. That weirdo form tutor never notices 'owt. I called your name out in register, like always."

"German were a laugh," goes Becky. "Gonna have a right laugh this year. Rest were borin'."

I goes, "OK. Now for the serious stuff. Food an' entertainment. I'll skank some food, Becky the glue, Tracey the cider."

Becky's like, "But they know me!"

"So?! They know me! Be quick! Tracey'll act as decoy."

Tracey won't skank owt, but she's loyal. She's well pretty, too, and cute, like butter wouldn't melt. She can wrap the security guards round her little finger. And the store detectives – we know who they are. We have this routine. The three of us goes into Mycock's the late shop, but separate like. Becky goes to near back of shop, actin' *dead* suspicious an' dodgy. She's pickin' up this an' that, puttin' stuff in pockets, openin' packets, lookin' round all dodgy. 'Course the trick is, she's clean, she hasn't nicked owt, but the detective and owner have their eyes on her. It's true, they do know her, the more they do, the more they're out to get her. But they don't know me. So I fills a big bag with food, tins, bread, biscuits, packets, all legit lookin' like. Meanwhile Becky's bein' all dodgy, all eyes are on her. Then on my sign, Tracey approaches the checkout geezer, detective, dogsbody, whoever's between me an't door. She flutters her eyelids and asks some sweet an' innocent question: "Oh, excuse me please, I'm shopping for my mummy and can't seem to find any wholegrain flour, can you help me please?" She asks about something she knows is at the opposite end of the shop, Becky's still makin' a right fuss, I walk out calmly with my shopping bag. Never failed. Today it works a treat and I have time for some sweets by the checkout. Out of the shop, I leg it from the precinct, Tracey follows soon and we meet up around the corner. Becky's usually ten minutes later. We take it in turn to skank the glue from the hardware shop. The owner's ninety-five so it's a doddle. The booze is Tracey's job, again 'cause she looks so sweet. We stand outside the offy and pick a young lad goin' in for himself. "Excuse me, could you please buy me a bottle of white cider for my friends, they're too shy to ask. Oh please... I'll give you an extra 50p..." It works. Only Tracey can do it. I don't talk, and if Becky did it, they'd run a mile. But things work with Tracey.

So we're sorted. Food, glue, booze, and it's only 4:30.

The food is for home. It's boring, nicking things like biscuits, I know. But Dad needs the housekeeping money for booze. It has to be that way. *I* can't nick his booze, it's always hidden away behind counters. *He* couldn't nick anything to save his life, he's too useless and clumsy, he'd get caught first time. So we made a deal; he spends the housekeeping money on his booze, it's just about enough. I skank the necessities, as people call them. It's a funny way of doing it, but it's OK.

The glue is what gets us going. Every time. We do glue, nail varnish, aerosol, lighter fuel...It gives you a quick high, lasts about an hour. That'll do me. Tracey won't do it. But that's OK. Becky and I take turns; one pulls the plastic bag over the other's head while the other inhales. You gotta be careful – too little and you don't get a hit, too much and you faint. I've fainted before, it's scary. I know people who've been in real trouble, the aerosol froze their throat and they choked. You can puke and choke on your puke if you pass out. This time it's cool for us. I love the dizzy, tingly feeling as you drift away.

The booze is to keep us topped up. I like this bit 'cos Tracey joins us. We sit among the bins by the back of the precinct and take swigs from this big plastic bottle of

The Mountain

strong white cider. It's foul, it probably tastes worse than the glue, but it's well strong and it keeps us topped up.

We do this most days 'till about 6. Then Tracey has to go. Becky can do what she likes but I have to see to Darren and Dad so she leaves with me.

It's a long walk back up to Coombs Moss Park but we're all three high so we don't mind. I leave my mates at the entrance. They've never been inside the park and they don't want to. I don't want them too, an' all. It stinks. They make their way up past the park to the estate at the top of the hill. For me, it's home.

I walk up the muddy path, past skips and rubbish dumps on either side. Barrels, tins of paint, beaten up prams, tyres, bin liners and old newspapers line the path. There's a smell of burning rubber. Dogs and cats fight, women shout, kids scream, only the lazy bastard men can't be heard (yet) 'cos they're all either out getting wrecked or they're asleep. Our caravan is right at the top of the hill in the park, miles away from the others. That's OK by me. As I climb up the last bit my heart sinks. The stone has been moved to one side of the door and it looks like a light's on. The moon is already out and it's getting dark. I walk up the last few steps to the door and now I can smell it. Dad's not back yet. Thank God.

Darren is though. Thievin' little bastard. He's got a Nintendo, some sweets and a magazine. I ruffle his hair, that's all we do as signs of affection, but he knows and I know. We have an hour or so before our lives are turned upside down.

So although I'm still high, I got to wash his and my school things in the sink, then make tea – beans then biscuits – then tidy up as best I can, then empty out the loos and put sheets up at the windows for curtains. I don't mind too much though, it's OK, 'cos I'm just enjoyin' the peace before Dad gets back. I even have time for a little wash and change into my black top and jeans. Dad may not want tea, depending on how bad he is. Darren and I eat as much

27

as we can, then I tidy up (again), then I lie back on my bed and grab a bit rest.

I am listening to my Walkman. I shut my eyes and everything disappears for a while. I am still dizzy from the glue and the weirdest patterns dance in front of my eyes. My body is all pins and needles. I feel numb but strangely warm and comfortable. For the next few minutes, nothing else matters or is real an' I drift away.

Nothing else matters. Darren has gone, Dad has gone, school has gone. I have gone to another place, where I can be alone forever. The shapes in my head are merging and slowly going crazy. Black inside an' outside.

A massive crash jolts the whole caravan. I think it's going to collapse. Even with my headphones on I can hear the deafening crash of footsteps and furniture being kicked over. I reach to turn on the lights. Dad is back, much later than usual which means much worse than usual. He is soaking. The rain has soaked through his shirt, he's lost his coat, he's been sick everywhere and he's bleeding. Snot and spit crust his cracked lips. Darren blinks in the light like a scared rabbit. I almost feel sorry for him. But I can see: this time Dad's so far gone he won't cause us any trouble. It's better like this. He doesn't have the energy to shout or to hit us. He couldn't swing a frying pan or chuck a plate to save what's left of his life.

We've done this before. Darren and I get out of our beds, lay Dad flat on his, pull off his trousers and his wet shirt and I wash him down with a damp tea towel. His hair is muddy, one eye is bleeding and he seems to have lost another tooth. If he had a wallet when he went out it's gone now. He's making all kinds of noises and grunting and groaning, and we know that the night will be disturbed. But for now I'm almost relieved. No-one gets hit or sworn at, nothing gets broken as far as I can see, and he can't eat so we've got extra left for tomorrow. It's so bad it's good.

28

Chapter 3

The first few weeks have passed in my new life and nothing has happened to convince me that this is a job that I want to do. The pupils are brutish louts who smell and are loud, the staff mostly appear to have no time for them and nothing in common with them. For all the fine ideals in the school's mission statement, I find little of it put into practice and no-one will admit to being at all interested in the kids' welfare. Ironically, for I am still naïve enough to be interested, the pupils bully me at least as much as each other. Because I try to be kind to them and understand them and I don't wear a pinstriped suit with five ball-point pens in the breast pocket, they see me as a chink in the armour rather than a potential ally. As such I am generally acknowledged to be fair game. I was told by Anthony that there was a two-week "honeymoon" period at the beginning of term, during which the pupils would 'size me up.' I feel that I was perhaps not up to scratch during this period, and that the rest of the marriage will prove a disappointment to them.

My 5th year class are hell on earth already, but I am starting to mess things up with other classes as well. Towards the end of my 2nd year German class I pause and say:

"Well, any questions?"

The usual silence follows, but then a small girl with a ruddy face like a pig's says:

"Sir, are you German?"

I hesitate, a technique I should avoid like the plague, but don't. I may as well have declared open season for irrelevant questions and comments. They come with a speed which surprises me:

The Mountain

"Don't be gay! How can he be German if he lives here?"

"Sir, are you married?"

"I hate Germans, they bombed my auntie's chippy!"

"Sir, what's your first name?"

"Sir, you got any kids?"

"Course he don't, he's gay!"

"Sir, you got a girlfriend?"

"What's she like?"

This last question prompts predictable laughter. Although the questions are plainly directed at me, the class don't wait for me to answer, but seem to have as much fun filling in the answers as in waiting for any I might give. In fact, just like my 5th year, they are ignoring me.

My pastoral skills as a form tutor are no better; the only blessing is that form time in the morning is mercifully short. The form wander in and out at will, and my case is not helped by the fact that many of them are also in my nightmare German 5B2. I only noticed the other week that that moody girl who won't talk, who was the source of all the trouble, is in my form, too. When she turns up. She still won't talk, but her friend answers for her. A nice, rather large girl in the front row called Tracey keeps me organised: "Sir, where's the register? Sir, tell them to wait outside. Sir, here comes Mr Gillespie. Sir, you do absences in red pen, not pencil. Don't leave any blanks..." She is like a dripping tap in one way, yet the only sign so far that someone cares.

Anthony and Gillespie are both on my back – sort of. Anthony doesn't really care and is too lazy to do much about anything. He is a little embarrassed by the fuss I am causing, as I am gaining a reputation amongst staff and pupils of being completely useless as a disciplinarian. He usually walks away or says something inconsequential like "It'll all come out in the wash." Gillespie, on the other hand is inspired; he is a man on a mission, a dog with a

30

bone, and I am his 'cause célèbre.' He is going to make me into a proper teacher, one that the children fear and loathe. If ever I should succeed, it will all be thanks to *him.*

My evening sessions in the pub are becoming more and more regular, and I am getting to know some people in that way. Anthony has stopped coming. One evening I say:

"Who were those two young ladies who joined us on that first evening?"

The sound of three people simultaneously spitting out their beer is the first clue that I have said something funny. Geoff Lennox is the first to recover. He wipes foam from his beard and says:

"Young ladies! That's a good one! First time they'll have been called that! Ever! Two witches, more like! If you're going to survive here with us, Nigel, stop being so bloody polite!"

David Stanton looks at him, then at me, as if to suggest I've been let off lightly.

"I think you'll find," he begins, "that you are referring to my colleague, Judy Hartington, and her…friend Eleanor Whiting. The words 'young' and 'lady' don't automatically spring to mind, in the opinion of this humble observer. A brace of fraudulent, bogus new-age sorcerers perhaps. Eleanor must the biggest skiver known to the teaching profession – a proper little *malade imaginaire.* And if I were you," he pauses, the air pregnant with the expectation of these next few words, "I wouldn't really trust them."

"Oh, they're OK," counters Geoff. "Bit false, that's OK. They're inseparable – we think they share everything: taste in houses, furnishings, food, men - "

"Opinions," interrupts Lou, who has been silent so far.

31

The Mountain

"Well *I,*" resumes David, "don't trust them. They are false. False friends."

I am intrigued and decide to fish a little more. It hasn't occurred to me so far that there could be divisions and factions among the teaching staff. Thus far I thought of them as one great homogenous dehumanised mass. This is fun. I probe further, my naivety still intact:

"What's John Gillespie like?"

"Hah!" I'm not sure who says it, if it is even a word, that is, but the reaction is nearly as pronounced as that which greeted my 'young ladies' *faux pas.* I think perhaps I have stumbled on their pet hate, and it heartens me. Geoff is again quickest with his finger on the buzzer, showing a mental nimbleness I would not automatically have attributed to him.

"Pompous git."

"Jumped up little twerp," confirms Lou. "Thinks he owns the place. Kids hate him. *Hate* him. They fear him, mind. He's a disciplinarian, good to have on your side. Just don't ask us to like him."

"The Head?"

"Slimy." This is Geoff again, but the others quickly concur; it is unanimous.

"You will find," David informs me, "that he is a good PR man with the parents – you could never accuse Gillespie of that, he's too savage. But again, I don't trust the man. Watch his *eyes.* He has a public face and a private face. I don't know how supportive he'd be of you if you needed it."

This is intriguing because, as he speaks, David's eyes dart nervously around the room, never resting for a second. They crave the attention of the listener, they need reassurance.

"What about Anthony?"

This time they laugh. At least they agree with their reactions; it is like listening to one voice.

The Mountain

"Nice guy, bit ineffective," says Lou, and I sniff damningly faint praise. David is more forthright:

"He's useless. He gave up caring years ago. Kids don't respect him, he can't control them, results are bad. He's a bit of a stock character in the staffroom, you'll find. The affable old cricket-loving buffoon."

"They're all false, nothing is real," adds Lou cryptically.

At around seven the two young ladies pop in for a quick drink. They are dressed in the latest chic, which in the case of one of them could be mistaken for the curtains in my flat; they are going to the theatre. They join us very briefly, a couple of gin and tonics to give gravitas to the table bearing our empty pint glasses. They are busy and in a hurry.

"How are we, ladies?" enquires David, apparently sincerely.

"We're gid," comes the reply from the first one, Eleanor. "We're off to the theatre?"

"Terrific. What to see?"

"*Of Mice and Men*?" Eleanor has this antipodean, or is it transatlantic, affectation of making everything into a question, even though it isn't a question and I have decided she hails from no-where more exotic than Nottingham. She turns to me. "So how do you like skill?"

"Pardon?"

"Our skill. Where you work."

"Oh. Ah, yes, fine."

"You look old," says the other, Judy, to me. This amuses my companions.

"Thanks," I venture.

"Old for a probationer, she means," qualifies Eleanor, the smaller and more garishly dressed of the two. "But she thinks you have something cute about you, you'll find out soon enough..."

33

The Mountain

I barely have time to express my thanks but the two socialites are out of the door, having been whisked onwards to their next engagement. The others at the table smile knowingly.

I am enjoying the free time in the pub, and find our interchanges oddly reassuring. The same cannot be said for the days in between them, which are a grind. I can't do anything with any but the very youngest of my classes. They don't hate me – they have a lot of fun with me – but my ideals have already disappeared and I hate them. I want to be something real to them but at the moment I am just a toy. Will they only respect me if I turn into someone like Gillespie (who *does* hate them)?

I can't sleep. I drink a lot with my new friends, I drink a lot anyway, but it doesn't help me sleep. My mind races, it darts from topic to topic like David's mad eyes, never focussing on any one thing. Then, just when I am about to sleep, little devils surface and keep me awake. In the dead of night, devils dance inside my head. The night is playing tricks on me. I am afraid. I don't sleep and can't rest because I have known this fear before.

Associations run freely in my mind; the slightest thing sparks off a memory. For example, when I fry bacon in butter, I am reminded of France. Chopping an onion in a certain direction makes me think of a tram near the Universitätsplatz in Heidelberg. The preparation of a mushroom omelette can almost persuade me that I am back at university, about to make love for the first time with my first ever girlfriend in a dingy bedsit. Earlier this evening I made what I thought of as a fairly prosaic snack of bacon butties.

I was in France. I studied for nearly two years, doing a doctorate on a comparison between Louis Aragon and Georges Brassens. Star-crossed lovers, uneasy bedfellows with nothing in common but their anarchists' souls and their hopeless love, it was a project doomed to failure from the start. I sat at a typewriter in a barn in Marthelod, in the Alps. I didn't trouble the staff much at Chambéry University library, I spent day upon day in the barn, dreaming. One day while dreaming I fell in love with an Italian girl, and I wished I could undream her. But in the days when I slept, my dreams were master.

Some weeks later I met her; she was real. Marcia Bianchi, tiny, raven-haired, beak-nosed, from an extended Savoyard-Italian family. Brothers and relatives everywhere. I don't even know how we met. We spent most of the year together, until the events that split us up, the events that stopped me from sleeping and dreaming. That happened much later.

This is when the fear came. I was in bed with Marcia, at her flat not at the barn. The bed was far too big for our small bodies, we splayed and kicked around in it like two solitary coins in a wallet. What was it warned us to be restless that night? I remember hearing four o' clock, seeing the morning light's first tentative beams, then the door being kicked open, her estranged husband Paolo and two minders, covered in blood and drenched in booze after the weekly 'bal'. Nothing in my life so far had prepared me for the fear I felt. "Tire-toi, l'anglais." said Paolo. I had sprained my ankle the previous week but still moved with incredible speed. I was out of bed and dressed before the three 'sales gueules' had entered the room properly. Marcia in a daze, Marcia asking me to stay…Months later I understood why. There was menace in the very words which I took to reassure me: "J'suis pas en colère avec toi, l'anglais…"and the last words of the henchman, as he shook my hand were icy: "à un de ces quatres."

These are the people I like:
Geoff Lennox, PE teacher. He is in his third year of teaching. He is small and thin, with a patchy black

beard and beady little eyes. He loves football, which somehow seems to bring out the (distant) Scottish ancestry to which he lays claim.

David Stanton, English teacher. He is in his second year of teaching. He never says anything in a straightforward way; I wonder if he specialised in circumlocution at university. He is tall, slim, and very opinionated. He sincerely feels that we, and for all I know others, benefit from having heard his political opinions, his interpretation of the latest political machinations, his stance on the latest news story. He says things like: "And who's paying for them, anyway? I'll tell you who; the likes of you and me, that's who!" His eyes dart quickly and nervously around when he is speaking.

Lou Miles, Business Studies teacher, so he only teaches older kids. He too is in his second year of teaching. He pretends to be very Bohemian and alternative. He has longish black hair, four days' worth of beard the whole time, and an earring at weekends. He says things for effect and always tries to be controversial. He says things that no-one understands, although they don't understand him in a different way from the way they don't understand David. He says things like: "My room is filling up with guitars and dust."

And those are the people that I like. The people I don't like are:

Anthony Marshall, my head of department. He is patronising in his attempts to be protective.

John Gillespie, head of 5th year. I have already decided that he thinks he is much more important than he is. He says things like: "The bell *has* gone, ladies and gentlemen", or "The children are waiting."

Kenneth White, Dr White, the head. He is slimy and oily. He speaks so differently to pupils, staff and parents that you might think there were three of him.

Judy Hartington (English) and Eleanor Whiting (Science) are two relatively young teachers who hang around with our group and I don't yet know which category to put them in. They are friendly with us up to a point but are a bit aloof. Their distant manner gives the clear impression that they think they are better than us. They wear designer clothes. Judy has this unplaceable accent which changes like a chameleon to ape and pick up the verbal mannerisms of whoever she is speaking to. So in conversation with Dr White, she sounds slimy and sinister, whereas with David Stanton she speaks like a long-winded pompous ass.

I like Thursday. Most of my devils have gone, and left me, by Thursday, which is near enough to the end of the week to not make much difference. So it is that on Wednesday nights I sleep quite well, certainly better than on any other work night. In what could be termed convoluted logic, I therefore begin to think of Thursday evening as the start of my weekend (I can survive like this: a weekend that lasts for four days, that is until the devils come flying back on Sunday evening) and have arranged to meet my new friends in the pub as near to 3.55 as is possible.

Geoff, David and Lou are already in the Swan with Two Necks. They look as if they've never been away. It is Thursday and Geoff is talking about football. He has remembered his Celtic heritage, appropriately so as Celtic is the subject of his conversation and the reason for his excitement. He is very agitated as he pronounces:

"Jackie Dziekanowski". Once again I wonder if this is a part of some pre-arranged code, but I am learning a little about how these people talk and I wait.

"Four goals!! Four!! And they still lost!"

I piece together the clues. It is Thursday, Celtic have just played the home leg of their tie against Partizan Belgrade, and all has not gone according to plan. Geoff is struggling to get his words out in anything like a coherent

manner, or even in the correct order, so he lets the
newspaper on the table in front of him do the work.

"Look, I'll read the match report. 'Celtic 5 –
Partizan Belgrade 4. (Partizan Belgrade go through on
away goals rule.) Last night at Parkhead saw the most
incredible night of European football in living memory. In
a rollercoaster match, the Bhoys came from behind to lead,
thanks to two finely taken chances by Dziekanowski only
for Belgrade to equalise within minutes, a pattern which
repeated itself midway through the second half, with
further goals from Dziekanowski and Djurivski. Walker
and Dziekanowski appeared to guarantee Celtic's passage
into the second round with goals in the 65th and 80th
minute, but in the 87th minute Scepovic scored to make it 5-
4 and put the tie beyond Celtic's reach, Partizan going
through on the away goals rule.

Celtic were always chasing the tie, as they needed
to win by a margin of two clear goals in spite of having
gained an away goal in the first tie in Mostar a fortnight
ago. Nevertheless Celtic's heroics on the night,
particularly those of Polish striker Jackie Dziekanowski,
were so nearly rewarded. This must be the first player in a
European tie to score four goals and still be on the losing
side. Afterwards manager Billy McNeil said: 'We were
given a mountain to climb on four occasions. On the first
three occasions we succeeded, but the fourth was simply
asking too much. I'm very proud of the lads and their
efforts, in the end we ran out of steam and ran out of time.
It's a cruel way to lose a tie, but we'll be back next year.'"

The evening session is an extended one, befitting
the beginning of an extended weekend. At 11.30 we
stagger homewards, noisily and uncertainly. I leave my
companions by my flat but hesitate before going in. It is
my weekend, yet I doubt whether I shall sleep. I gaze up at
the sky, imagining the stars concealed behind the rain.
Over to the north I discern the vague grey shape of Mam

The Mountain

Tor, shivering mountain. Mam Tor and the Great Ridge. There is something uneasy about its presence.

Many years ago an eloping couple were brutally murdered in Winnat's Pass, under the watchful eye of the shivering mountain. It watched them flee, seemed to guard them until within minutes of safety, then mocked their efforts as it allowed their pursuers to catch up with them. A young eloping couple were about to reach their destination when a group of five miners ambushed, robbed and murdered them. In an eery development, Clara, the young bride, foresaw the double murder in a dream. The young couple Allan and Clara were followed out of an inn and up the treacherous pass by the group of miners. On being attacked Clara fainted and could only cry out "My dream, my dream." Allan was murdered with a pick-axe, then Clara, in spite of her pleas for mercy. The murderers did not dare bury the bodies for the next three days. They were never brought to justice but all lived wretched lives, one committing suicide and two killed by the vengeful mountain herself; another one was haunted and given to thoughts of suicide and the last one confessed to the double murder before he died.

Until three hundred years ago the Great Ridge was used for funeral processions, the gruesome 'danse macabre' re-enacted by goblins and sprites in the shimmering moonlight. Mam Tor looms large, a sombre presence by day and by night, there to remind men of what they have done and should not have and to taunt them for what they should have done but have not. I look onto the obscure shape of sandstone and shale but can discern no expression. I am going into my flat, but without understanding why I feel very uneasy. I try to sleep under the vigilant, unrestful eye of the shivering mountain.

Chapter 4

The time I hate most is the weekend. I know it's weird. I hate school, I never go, but it's the weekends I really can't stand. During the week, I don't see Dad, I hardly see Darren or the caravan. On Saturday morning they're all three together in my face, and it does my head in.

If Dad could be a proper piss-head it'd be one thing. But every now and then he has to go all '*family*', like he cares, like he's the head of this family unit and like he makes a difference. It's crap and he does it for his own dignity, not for us. At least when he's wrecked in the evening he's not being a hypocrite. But his every now and thens are on a Saturday morning and it does my head in.

He goes, "Right, let's get this place all ship-shape," as if you could ever make a difference to our little dump of a caravan. All the military-like phrases and dignity in the world couldn't make this place ship-shape, or any other kind of shape. But he has us up at 9, which must be a punishment for him too, and we're emptying bins, sweeping floors, cleaning windows and dusting surfaces like we're expecting a royal visit. He's business-like; you can tell he's business-like 'cos he's wearing the kind of corduroys other people's dads sometimes wear and a shirt with no puke stains.

This farce lasts for two or three hours sometimes – there's not even enough stuff to clean to fill that time, for God's sake. That doesn't matter though. We keep going for Dad's dignity and his conscience. This is what we do so that, for three hours each week, he feels that he's a proper dad at the head of a proper family. It's pathetic, but

The Mountain

it keeps him sane. At about 12 he gives us each 50p, which
is a joke 'cos we have more money than him and always
nick things anyway, and then he heads off into town with
his child benefit and income support, if he has any left.
I've followed him before, but I don't need to, he's like
clockwork. Bookie's first, then a drink or two in the Red
Lion opposite, then back to the bookie's, then the proper
drinking starts with a bottle of cheap Scotch from the offy,
then the bookie's again 'till his mates hit the Lion just after
the footie results. By this time he's broke, by about 7 he's
completely wrecked but his mates'll buy him drink 'till
chucking out time 'cos it's a laugh. He'll stagger in around
midnight, too trashed to stand and having blown a week's
money in one day, but his conscience is clear 'cos we tidied
our skanky little caravan and he gave his kids enough
money for a bag of chips between them for dinner and tea.

It's as well that Darren and I can fend for
ourselves. We breathe a sigh of relief when Dad's out the
place. Darren goes to a mate's for dinner, where at least
he'll get fed. Mostly I run. I'll do some glue or a bong
with some of the kids on the Park, then I don't feel like
eating. The high'll keep me goin' 'till tea-time. I go into
town and meet up with my only two mates, we'll hang
around, get some booze, skank or, if I'm feelin' rich, buy
some food, then I'm back to feed the little brat around 6; if
not, he's got enough for some chips – they sell us the left
overs from the used pans for cheap. I prefer the chips
option, 'cos then I can stay in town an' get really wrecked.
Why should Dad have all the living?

Sunday is mostly the same, but more dead. Dad
used to get up early an' go to church, which really made
me laugh. Nowadays I guess even his conscience don't
need that. What he does need is sleep, 'cos the bags under
his eyes which used to be grey are now black, and the lines
around his eyes have got lines. Plus, when he's asleep he's
no trouble, if you can stand the grunting and the smell. It's
a small price to pay.

41

The Mountain

When he's awake and hung-over, he's hell. For some reason he saves this kind of thing for Sundays. His temper is vile, he'll smack Darren for nowt, he used to smack me but I think he's embarrassed now. But his tongue's as bad; he'll call me all the names if his dinner's not ready after he's been to the Legion late Sunday morning. Darren gets slapped if the place isn't tidy, if the water runs cold, if he's just sittin' there at the wrong time. Darren stays quiet, he's a tough little sod, but I can see the hate and resentment. He'll take it out on someone else, a shopkeeper, an old lady, a wimp at school, the teachers…That's not fair but neither's Dad lashing out at him 'cos he's miserable and hung-over. None of this is fair, but what can you do?

The first song by Morrissey that I listened to after The Smiths split was last year, called *Everyday is like Sunday*. I don't even like it, but it says something about my life. *Our* life. Grey, inside an' out. But I don't even like Morrissey, I hate him. He's broken up the one thing I cared about. I used to love him, with his quiff and his funny way of standing. With flowers that looked like they were growing out of him. He always looked so sad. Well now he's playing big stadiums and acting like he lives in America. He means nothing to me now. I liked him before things got too big, while he was still something I could relate to, not a superstar. While he was still real. I liked him when he sang things like *Half A Person*. Because that's me: I'm still 15, I'm only 15 but it's still about me. It's me, and it's real, not poncing about in flash cars and swimming pools. The day The Smiths finished, that was it for me; that was when I stopped talking to people.

Something else happened that year: Eddie died. I was with him the whole time, everyday, I used to look out for him, and I turned my back and he died. Kids around us on the Park now, they do drugs, glue, lighter fuel; they

42

drink, they smoke, they nick cars and joyride. Eddie did nothing, and he died.

It was just before Christmas, I can remember exactly, it was Saturday 12th December 1987. It had been unusually cold, snow was lying and everything was frozen. Eddie had gone with some mates in their car to a party just out of town. His mate Robbie, two years older than him, had just passed his test and had borrowed his dad's car for the evening. About 11 that night, I got the most terrible headache and buzzing in my ears. I woke up in bed in a cold sweat – the bed clothes were wet through. When I closed my eyes lights flashed inside my head. The buzzing turned to ringing, loud ringing. I couldn't close my eyes for the pain, and the lights inside my head were brighter than if I had my eyes wide open. So I sat there, my heart beating so loud I could hear it, until the doorbell rang.

Mum answered. The police. I can hear every word as if it were yesterday. The words haunt me every day – still. "Mrs Lomas? Is your husband in? We're sorry to have to tell you…" My heart jumped as a woman's voice took over. I rushed to the mirror and stared at my own red face, as if that would help. As if that would delay them telling. "Mrs Lomas, are you the mother of Edward Lomas, d.o.b. 12/11/72? Mrs Lomas, we have some bad news. There's been an accident. The car-"

I can do the rest myself; I do most days. It never helps. The car he was in skidded on black ice at the top of the hill coming into town, just by the golf-course. It spun off the road, rolled down an embankment, smashed into a dry-stone wall. All four passengers were killed at the scene of the accident. They had to be cut free, but it was too late. They weren't speeding, although the driver may have taken the sharp bend in too high a gear. Span completely out of control – no other vehicle was involved. The driver hadn't even had a drink. The time of the fatal accident was 22.59.

My mum let out a low pitched moan, like a growl, like some animal. My dad said nothing for ages. Darren

The Mountain

was asleep. That left me. I just sat in front of the mirror for ages, looking at my red face, and my eyes. The rims of my tired eyes grew redder until they seemed to merge with the red of my face. And the silence in the house was unbearable.

Eddie was the one person I ever loved and he left a hole. He was two years older than me but you wouldn't know it. He was nice to me and accepted me as his mate. He let me hang with his mates. He got me into the music and never once told me to get lost. He let me look out for him, too. He looked out for me in school, and with Dad. I can see his face now, inside my head. Tall and slim, loads of curly blond hair everywhere and a long, sad-looking face. But those eyes used to understand. They used to understand *me,* and it makes me want to cry.

It also makes me angry. Why did Eddie die? He was perfect, never did nothing wrong to anyone. And the day he died, our life as a family died.

We didn't always live in a caravan on the Park. We had a really nice house in town, it wasn't a council house. I used to love it. It was warm. My room was next to Eddie's, and I used to hear his music, to listen to his music, like I was in his room with him. I used to snuggle up warm in bed and dream I was in his room. We were safe in that house. But when Eddie died Mum flipped, and a bit of all of us died. She used to sit all day and just look out of the bay window in the front room. The silence in that front room was unbearable. All you could hear was the mantelpiece clock ticking. That was all you heard in the house, after Eddie died. Mum must have found it unbearable, too, 'cos she left not long after Christmas. She made sure we had what we needed. I got an amp for my bass, Darren got his Nintendo. Eddie was to have gotten a new guitar. It stayed in his room unopened. Mum and Dad went out to the Legion on New Year's Eve, the first time they'd been out together since the accident. There was a sadness in Dad's eyes as they left the house that night. He

The Mountain

knew. Mum stayed all New Year's Day but then the next day, the 2nd, she was gone. No note, nowt. She had got tired of coming home to a house where love was dead. She was gone and Dad knew why.

Our family died soon after. Mum disappeared without a trace. Dad started drinking the whole time. Darren went really wild for a while, uncontrollable. He's still bad now. I just withdrew from the world. The only person who really meant anything, who was real to me, was gone.

One night after Mum had gone I did a weird thing. Darren was in bed, Dad was God knows where getting himself trashed. For the first time since the accident, I went into Eddie's room. Everything was exactly as he'd left it that Saturday evening, I know 'cos I'd been in the room with him. It was eerie. Old guitar out, same CDs lying about. Same CD in the machine. The room hadn't even been cleaned. I put the CD on – *The Queen is Dead.*

Eddie didn't even get to be in a coma. His death was so final he didn't even have that little tiny glimmer of extra time, that little extra chance. No-one asked anyone if they thought he'd pull through. No-one asked that about Darren; there was no point. I couldn't listen any more. My eyes, my face were wet with tears, it was just too painful. I put on another CD – the track was *There is a Light That Never Goes Out*. I felt much better – I wished I could have died by his side.

I put on his T shirt and shorts, still under his pillow but they'd gone cold. His pillow, his bed was cold. I put on his things, lit one of the many candles around his room, and lay in his bed listening to that one track all night long.

I stayed there all night, and no-one noticed.

After that the family really started to go to pieces. Dad was doing nothing but drinking. He got time off work,

45

sick leave, but one day he got breathalysed driving our car
– at 9 in the morning. He failed the breath test and failed
so badly he got banned for two years. That lost him his job
driving diggers for the council. It wasn't long before that
lost us the house, he couldn't keep up mortgage repayments
on no money and Mum had worked too. Mum had a
decent job in an office and had really been the
breadwinner. Now Dad was left with us, no money, no job
and soon no house. He didn't even seem to care. He just
drank and drank. The house got repossessed in March of
that year, the week of my 14th birthday. As we were
moving out, Dad wanted me to know he was making one
last effort, he'd bought me a leather guitar case. We were
in the caravan, freezing, before the end of March. But I
had a guitar case.

Eddie wasn't just the only person I cared about,
but he introduced me to the only thing I care about (apart
from running) – music. (I don't care about the booze and
glue; I don't care about the bongs. They're just escape
routes.) He played in a band, I used to sit in and listen to
him on lead. He could do Johnny Marr's jangly guitar bits,
even the complicated ones. He made me want to be in a
band. So, when his band's bass player got a new bass, he
and I put together all our cash and bought his old one for
£25. It wasn't a good one, it sounded terrible, but now I
had a guitar like Eddie. He showed me where the notes
were and taught me a couple of chords. That long summer
holiday when I was 13, before everything went bad, he
taught me a bit each day, and always something new.

At the beginning of my third year, Eddie decided I
was ready and asked Mr Brant, Head of Music, if I could
have lessons. Brant was like, "Her? What? Who? You're
not serious!" Eddie was like, "Why *not* her?" I was proud
of the way he stuck up for me. Brant and the other teachers
had decided I was nothing but trouble by this time (I still
talked to them at this time, just about) and he didn't want
me skulking around the music practice rooms putting

people off. Eddie stuck to his guns, going "She's good! She's got potential!" Luckily there was another music guy, Mr Fletcher, quite young and less of a dork than Branty. He was like, "We'll give her a trial. Ten lessons. You can plug into our P.A. here and see what noise you can make."

I was nearly happy. The Smiths had just split but Eddie had got me an instrument and I could play a bit. For two, three months I was nearly happy.

So now I do music. I don't talk, but I do music. I still have the bass and bass amp, we had to sell Eddie's guitars and gear so in a way I feel it's up to me to continue. I don't love it any more, not like I used to. I'd be lying if I said I still loved the music. I don't love anything. But I do it. I keep doing the music. This is the band:

Will Woods: lead guitar. Will is Becky's elder brother, a 6th former. He was Eddie's mate. We sold him Eddie's two guitars and amp. He's not bad; can't do the jangly bits like Eddie and Johnny Marr, but who can? Long blond hair all over the place.

John Mellor: vocals. A really good singer. He was in the band with Eddie, so he understands. Also a 6th former. Tracey's boyfriend. Shortish hair, quite fit, if I cared about that kind of thing.

Rick Taylor: drums. Left school. Short, fat and a beard. Was also in the band with Eddie. I don't think he's that good, really.

Anna Lomas: bass. The other half of the rhythm section. Smiths' obsessive. Knows every chord to every song. Moody cow. Don't talk.

We're over at Rick's practising. We have a gig after school, end of October, the Friday night before half-term. It's gotta be good. I don't look forward to it, but I'll be there. Today (a Sunday; what other day?) we stink. Rick's slow coming in, so I'm leading him. Will's playin' too fast and in some funny key he seems to have made up.

The Mountain

Only John sounds good, except he's a bit too good. He's too *polished* for this music. We need a rougher edge.

We try a few songs but nothing sounds right. Songs like *Hand in Glove, What Difference Does it Make? That Joke isn't Funny Any More.* Rick should really lead me but he doesn't, so it all sounds wrong. Only the last song, *There is a Light That Never Goes Out*, sounds OK. We put it into the key of G for John's voice. Will plays the intro, summat like: C minor, A flat, B flat, then it's the first bars: C minor, A flat, B flat, E flat, A flat . It sounds real. We're getting good, just as we're about to stop. I love the bass on this track. It sounds good when I lead Rick, just half a beat ahead, for once it sounds right. Will's guitar sounds perfect; I'm totally relaxed as I stride out on bass. This is maybe the most sinister song in the world, and I find it totally relaxing and soothing. And just for a minute, I'm lying in Eddie's bed two years ago listening to this track over and over again all night long, only this time somebody notices. And just for a minute, today isn't Sunday at all and Eddie isn't really dead.

Chapter 5

"And designer *ideas,*" says Lou. "I think that's what gets me, really. I can take the fake hippy thing, I can," which coming from him is rich, "but it's all the Marks and Spencers, walnut and avocado salad, studied scruffiness, fake henna lifestyle that really gets me."

I agree. "Designer dresses, designer food, hair, makeup; I bet their *bijou* flats are filled with the latest designer furniture and little trinkets. It's all so …false."

"You," opines David, "have barely been here a month, and you're as cynical as we." I assume it is a compliment.

"It's just that I'm sensitive to falseness," I try to explain; I am probably making things worse. "There's such a lot of it everywhere." I think my words make a mark; naïve in their simplicity, they fail to elicit a sarcastic response. The silence is awkward, until Geoff breaks it by suggesting another round.

"Re vera, potas bene, O Geoff," quips David as Geoff makes his way to the bar. The silence is still uncomfortable.

"So, are you both…happy in your chosen vocation?" I ask after a pause.

"Vah!" replies David cryptically. "It pays the rent and keeps one out of mischief. One does what one can…"

Not to be undone, Lou is typically obscure.

"We all do what we can. Time trickles through our fingers until it fades."

I am relieved when Geoff returns with the drinks.

The Mountain

My first year class has started humming – I mean
really humming. They hum when my back is turned, when
I am writing on the board. When I face them their mouths
are, of course, shut, but there is still a low pitched
humming in the room. As I walk around the room, the
humming grows louder in the parts of the room in which I
am not. If I have the temerity to confront the class about
this, fifty-six large innocent eyes stare at me like hurt
puppies. But as soon as I have had my say, the humming
starts again.

In my 3rd year French class a pupil peels off the
rubber sealant from around the newly installed windows
and fashions it into quite a large ball, the properties of
which I only became fully aware of when he throws it
across the classroom. Made of pure rubber, it bounces
across the room like a dervish on a pogo-stick, the biggest
super-ball ever invented in room A7.

Gillespie has stopped following me around
everywhere, which is both good and bad; I can breathe
without him jumping down my throat with liberal amounts
of criticism and useful advice, but on the other hand when I
want a gorilla to maintain order in my classroom, which is
about twenty times a day, I am usually alone. Anthony is
so useless he might as well not exist, and in spite of what it
might sound like, Gillespie's office in A21 is nowhere near
my room A7, being two floors above and at the other end
of a long corridor.

This morning my form mob me outside A7, a
combination of their exuberant form of greeting and the
usual way in which they congregate outside a room. A
shrill shriek like a whistle cuts through the air like a flying
knife:

"You lot!! What do you think this is? A Zoo?!
Stand in a straight line *now* and stop behaving like louts at
a football match, or you will practise doing so at morning
break. *Now!!!*"

The Mountain

As the layers of adolescent are slowly peeled away, I am left in the middle, face to face with a diminutive bespectacled and mouse like creature; it is Miss Needham, the librarian. She looks completely harmless and meek, yet with one shriek she has tamed the hordes which I couldn't even keep at bay. To her credit, she looks very embarrassed at finding a member of staff in the middle of the chaos.

Once a month or so we have form period, when we get to sit with our form for over an hour and discuss something we're not even qualified to discuss, scant difference though that makes to anything. We are to discuss the community we live in. It is a sacred rule of establishments like this that there is absolutely no political bias to be introduced, but I have had enough of petty rules and in any case no-one listens to a word I say. I could stand on top of my desk and sing the manifesto of the National Front and no-one would notice a thing. So it is with careless abandon and on largely deaf ears that I indulge my cynicism with the remark:

"Of course, the politicians have left their mark on communities like this. They have grabbed at the very heart of it, wrenched it out and bled it dry." It is a crass bit of politicking which I would have been embarrassed of in my student days, and I am relieved when no-one responds.

At the end of the lesson there is the usual rugby scrum formation by the door, not least because they have timetabled this particular session for just before lunch. If I am honest, however, there is never a good time of day for me to be here. When I raise my head from its habitual position of in my hands I see that two pupils have stayed behind. It is Tracey, who is an alert and attentive form member and who I think feels sorry for me, and more surprisingly Anna, who won't talk.

51

The Mountain

"We thought that was cool, what you said."
Naturally it is Tracey speaking. "Our families hate the
politicians and what they did to us." She fixes me with her
large, brown, doe-like eyes, and then emits four words
which stun me:

"Anna says you're OK."

"How did it go, old chap?" My interlocutor is
now Gillespie, who feels he needs to support me after tutor
period. I want to say, surprisingly well, actually. The
furniture is intact and I made two friends by making a
cheap political point, but decide that this is perhaps not the
moment.

"You've got that weird lot with the self-elected
mute, haven't you?" I decide this isn't a quiz; the question
is rhetorical.

"Good God," chimes Anthony, and sundry
reactionary grunts emanate from corners of the staffroom.
"She's trouble. Bolshy little bitch. Ran out of my lesson in
the 3rd year. *Third* year!! Disappeared for days. Police
brought her back."

"Yes and we wish they'd spared themselves the
trouble," retorts Gillespie, not wishing to be outdone.
"Sullen, truculent, *nasty* little piece of work. What's she
doing in a place like this? She needs a good slap."

I lack the confidence, the experience and the belief
that I am right to counter any of this, and I feel wretched.
This is the first time in nearly two months that I have felt
anything going well in the classroom, that I have had any
positive response from any pupil, and it is being washed
away in a tide of old men's jaded cynicism. But wretched
though I feel, I also feel strangely elated at the words
"Anna says you're OK" and I want to know more.

As fortune has it I am to teach my 5th year
German class last thing today. Last thing in the day is
never a good time and Anna is completely non-

communicative. I have started playing a game of throwing little jokes into my lessons, not to court any kind of popularity but simply as an exercise in seeing whether anyone notices. Mostly they do not. I am talking to the class about how precise Germans are, not in itself the most interesting of topics. "Germans are very precise," I hear myself drone. "They don't ask 'what platform does the train leave from?' they ask 'what *track* does it leave from?' They don't ask 'what's on the television?' but 'what's *in* the television?' If asking about the cinema they-"

The door bursts open and the familiar figure of Gillespie enters the room. The class falls suitably silent. He holds a piece of paper importantly in his hand.

"Please read this," he says curtly.

"Why, what does it say?"

"It doesn't *say* anything, Mr Charon, it's a piece of paper." He thinks he has put me in my place; one or two of my more alert scholars are smirking. "But on it, you will find written a request for information as to the aptitude and effort of some of your charges in this very room. Please complete it as a matter of some urgency."

He leaves as suddenly as he arrived. The usual increase in volume marks his departure, but there is a definite underlying snigger. And then I say very quietly:

"He vould a good German make, zis Herr Killespie."

I think I see half a smile cross Anna's face. Half a smile, across half a face; does that make half a person? She is quick to recover and buries her face in her coat.

To say that I am making progress would be to overstate things, but I am forming a bond with one or two pupils as the weeks go by. I cannot really be said to be in control of any one of my classes, yet I feel that I am not loathed like Gillespie or disdained quite as much as Anthony. Two or three pupils hover around at the end of each lesson and sometimes they even talk to me. I have a feeling that they quite like my subversive quips and appreciate the fact that I am prepared to talk to them. A loud girl called Rebecca stays for a chat after German sometimes. Tracey seems to have a mission which is to protect me as a form tutor and she tries to administer my staff development single-handedly. Curiously, both are friendly with the self-elected mute, of whom I consequently see quite a bit but with whom I (obviously) have not exchanged any words. She dresses from head to toe in black and at times wears black make-up. The effect is a little disconcerting but interesting.

One registration Tracey is listening to a Walkman. I take it off her. The mute girl stares at me in panic, as if I have cut her life-support machine, and it's not even *hers.* I am simply being curious, and on hearing some dirge-like lament, enquire as to its authors. Tracey's eyes widen, astonished that I have not confiscated the item, but her recovery is quick.

"The Smiths," she replies. "Miserable, aren't they?" There is a pause; I don't really know what to answer for the best. Tracey looks at Anna. "My boyfriend John sings in a band that do mostly their stuff. Anna's in it too. They're doing a gig. Wanna come?"

"Well, I…"

She sighs. "You teachers!" I feel that I have heard that many, many times before. She looks old and wise as she turns to Anna. "They make polite noises, but they never come. None of them are interested. They're all the same."

"Stop," I say as they turn to leave. "I'm different." It is a feeble rejoinder but I feel it to be true. I'm not phoney, patronising, sadistic, psychopathic, judgemental or hopelessly out of touch just yet. Of course I don't say any of this, but I would like a chance to prove it. "Tell me when, I'll come."

The gig is on the last Friday before half-term, 'sometime around 9.30', in the leisure centre. Tracey is surprised when I say I'll attend, then I even more rashly arrange to buy her and her mates a drink before the show. Not in the Swan, it goes without saying, but in the euphemistically called students' pub (some call it a crèche) The White Hart. My own drinking companions in the Swan are decidedly luke-warm about the idea.

"Meeting *pupils?!*" Geoff is incredulous, as if I had said sabre-wielding aliens.

"If," begins David in a tone which by now is very familiar to me, "you want my advice, you'll steer well clear. Pupils and staff don't mix, that's all there is to it. Put up with them in your classroom, if you really must, but let that be an end to it. Keep the appropriate distance – what is it you Germanists say, 'Abstand'? Stand well back."

"Anyway they're a weird bunch," contributes Geoff. "All black and Gothic. And that not-talking girl; how weird is *that?*"

"It's a drink for Christ's sake," I defend myself weakly. "Not a sixties-style love-in."

Lou feels that this is his cue.

"The vibe is heavy," is his apparently irony-free advice. "You can't cut it, I can't cut it, just-"

"Oh, kid you just shut up, Lou, for God's sake!" This is Judy and, although I would never admit it to the others, she has a point; at times like these Lou's faux-hippy drawl is delivered at a rate of about ten words per minute. The long pauses are as irritating as the words, and as empty of meaning. "Just understand that there are things that you can't do. Everyone will know. Cut your ties with them at the end of the day. It's just not done." Eleanor shows her assent in the fashion of a nodding dog on the back window-ledge of a car.

There was a time when those last four words would have been a sure guarantee that I would do whatever it was that I was being warned against doing. For now, I am content to sulk into my beer.

The Mountain

In any event I have listened to The Smiths, thanks to Tracey, and I quite like them. They lack the mindlessness of some of the more extreme punk of last decade, and certainly are an improvement on the pompous swill that preceded that particular movement. The singer sounds pained and tortured, but he sounds as if he means it. He sounds real.

On the last Friday evening of half-term we all drink heavily in the Swan. I have half a term's teaching experience behind me and want to celebrate. I leave at about 7 and make my way home to my flat where I get changed. I am strangely nervous about this evening and drink quite a bit more after I've had a shower. I change into some non-teacher clothes and climb back up the long steep hill I have just descended.

The White Hart is a depressing-looking dive not fifty yards from the leisure centre. Two of its windows are boarded up with chipboard which in itself is heavily and unpleasantly graffitied. Three children who must be under ten gather in the doorway to shelter from the rain; they appear to be in charge of a howling infant in a pram. Around the corner a group of pre-pubescent youths gather for an illicit smoke. Some aggressive looking teenagers gathered in the doorway of the leisure centre play a game involving bottles and lots of broken glass. I look across the street at the twee middle-class lighting of the Swan with its coal fire and its leather sofas, and almost turn around and make for the comfortable conversation of my friends in the snug bar.

There is no game of strip-poker, no gaudily clad hooker propping up an out of tune piano, and no dark stranger with six o'clock shadow and a ten-gallon stetson firing bullets at the bar, but in every other respect the interior of the White Hart resembles what I imagine a wild west saloon to look like. The furniture is wooden, uncomfortable looking and minimalist. The lighting is garish and neon. There really is sawdust on the floor. Some old drunks in a corner are trying noisily to remember the rules of the card game they are playing. A madman and a very fat woman canoodle at the bar and sing bad old country and western songs very loudly. And, to complete the cowboy film effect, everyone stops what they are doing, falls silent, and turns round to stare at me when I make my entrance.

I half want to drawl: "Well, howdy folks," but decide instead on a short nod of the head as I approach the only table with familiar faces. These faces too, are contorted with the confusion of non-recognition in spite of my best efforts. The overall impression in the place is quite hostile.

"Hello," I say, trying to sound as relaxed as I can.

"Oh my God!!!" shrieks the usually angelic Tracey. Dressed up and with make-up on she looks five years older. "It's sir! You've come after all!"

"Nigel, please," I try to reassure her. Someone sniggers. Someone else says: "Making any plans?" in a silly tone of voice, but firstly I am quite drunk and secondly I have got used to hearing this over the years. I am so cool, nothing can throw me.

"Well, *Nigel,*" cries an even louder than usual Rebecca with undue emphasis. "So you've deigned to join us – there's a first. Brought any of your mates with you?"

"They're not my mates, well, not really. And no, I come alone. I come in peace."

The permanently silent Anna sits at the table looking as bored as if she were in a school assembly. I presume that this is her having fun. She looks much as she does in school, in fact, with blacker make-up and a whiter face, with an array of silver jewellery but otherwise she could be sitting in my form period. Opposite her sit two thoroughly disinterested and unimpressed looking girls who contrive to look even moodier than Anna does.

The Mountain

"Drink, anyone?" A flicker of interest manages to cross most of the faces at the table, but only a flicker. This is an initiation test which will require more than money to pass.

We drink more as the evening passes. We are joined by four or five hairy young men which only makes me feel more out of place. Amongst themselves, the youths are gregarious, rowdy, drunken; with me they clam up suspiciously, all inhibitions, shoe-gazing and folded arms. If anything this polarisation becomes more pronounced the more drink is consumed. The table splits into two clear factions, the noisy youths at one end and myself at the other.

I stand up, not quite sure whether to go to the bar again or to leave for the bourgeois sanctuary of the Swan, when Rebecca asks me:

"So, *Nigel,* d'you know The Smiths?"

This is my trump card.

"Yes, I do, actually."

"And do you… like them?"

I pause long enough to sound blasé.

"They're OK."

Now at last some of our group are paying attention.

"Just…OK? That's, like, it?"

"Oh, the music's good enough. I'm not too sure about the lyrics."

The shock on the face of the otherwise worldy-wise and apathetic youths is a pleasure to behold; I have the inspiration for an H.E.Bateman style of cartoon – *The Man Who Questioned The Superiorty Of The Smiths' Lyrics*. A bedraggled sweaty-looking boy cranes forward and from behind a hedge of hair enquires:

"You *what?!* Can you like, back that up?"

I am not familiar enough with the *oeuvre* of the group in question to justify my attention-seeking remark, and feel suddenly unveiled as a charlatan caught out of his depth trying to be cool with youths half his age. Even through my drunken haze I feel slightly ashamed. Tracey takes my silence as a sigh of non-comprehension, a mistake I frequently make in the classroom.

"He means, can you think of an example?"

"Thanks, Tracey, I'd be stuck without you." My sarcasm is only there to buy me time, but suddenly I have an inspiration. It's staring me in the face, it's all around me in these hostile, suspicious eyes. "Yes, yes as a matter of fact I think I can. What about that song about the teachers?"

I've stumped them; they are silent. I know the lyrics better than they do. I glow with pride.

"Sorry, man, you've lost me," concedes the hairy youth after some time for conferring.

"You know," I explain patiently. "The one that goes "Hang the teachers" fifty million times at the end."

There is another pause, nearly as long, with nearly as much conferring. Showing much more energy than I thought they had, the two sullen girls sitting opposite start to hoot with peals of raucous laughter, followed as if orchestrated by their male companions. Rebecca and Tracey look at me sadly, almost apologetically, then join in with *their* male partners. Only Anna remains impassive. The Swan seems an attractive option.

I get up to leave unnoticed. But as I reach the door, a presence is behind me. I turn and it is Tracey.

"Hey, don't go…"

"I'm sorry Tracey, it was a mistake my coming."

"Why? What's wrong?"

"Oh, for God's sake! You're sweet but I don't fit in. These aren't my people, this isn't my music. I'm a fraud, a big fake. I've got to go."

"Nigel! Don't be so quick to…compartmentalise people." I have never heard her, or any pupil at Chapelton Community College use such a big word.

"What did you say?"

The Mountain

"Who *says* you don't fit in?" She blushes. "*I'm* glad you came…"

"Yeah *right,*" I reply, hoping the intonation is as it should be.

"So's Anna."

The thought stops me momentarily in my tracks.

"Oh, Tracey, you know I doubt that, I really do. She and I have never even exchanged words, so I think the contribution I could make to her evening's happiness is somewhat limited, don't you?"

I feel bad for taking my frustration out on Tracey. But she's not as meek as she looks and retaliates with persistent determination.

"Don't be a clown. She likes you. Your reaction means you at least like her a bit. Buy her a drink."

"Not now."

"Then later. Come to the gig. She likes Heineken."

Tracey turns to go. She has made her point and has no reason to watch me wallow in self-pity. Then she faces me again.

"Oh, and it's 'DJ.'"

"What?"

"That song. *Panic*. It's the *DJ.*"

Chapter 6

The band is shaping up good. I didn't think it ever would, but it is. The opening chords to *Last Night I Dreamt Somebody Loved Me*, one of their last songs, sound great. They're electric.

Things at home are no better. Dad has given up and doesn't do a thing. He's asleep when I leave in the morning, out getting wrecked by the time I'm back in the evening. If it wasn't for Saturday morning we'd never see him, which has its good side. I have to do everything – cook, clean, get that thieving little bastard Darren ready for school and write notes for him when he hasn't gone. I even have to check his spellings which is a joke. Mostly they don't get done, but last week we got a snotty letter from the school –'we regret to inform you that your son/daughter Darren is behind with his spellings and we are moving him to the orange spelling group. Please endeavour to check that your son/daughter checks his/her spellings on a weekly basis and that you sign his planner. Please feel free to discuss this matter with us at a suitable date.' Of course I have to deal with the letter, not that I feel free to discuss anything with them.

School is weird. Gillespie still hates me and seems out to get me any chance he has. The others stay off my back, not him; recently it's been uniform. "Are those regulation earrings, young lady? Is that…*make-up* you're wearing? I'm not convinced about the length of that skirt, young lady. With health and safety regulations being what

61

they are – yet another area of school life that *I* have to deal with, as if I didn't have enough on my plate – *any* garment that length constitutes a health hazard. What if we had a fire?" For tiny-minded pettiness Gillespie takes some beating. I want to answer him back, to destroy his logic. I want to say: "*Health* hazard! Why can't you just say you don't like my clothes? Teachers wear dangly earrings and I haven't seen *them* getting caught in a lathe in the metalwork workshops. Our Science teacher wears a long skirt but she hasn't yet tripped over it and set the whole Chemistry lab on fire. And if there *was* a fire, wouldn't we all burn anyway? And if *you've* got so much on your plate, Mr Self-pitying martyr, then get off my case and that'll be one job less for you to fret about." Of course I don't say this; I'd just like to. I'd also like to smack him, but I can't really do that.

I can't relate to any of this. It's not real to me, any of it. Really, I'm just marking time, wasting away my life and counting the days 'till I can leave. Wishing the days away. There's nothing for me here.

Our new form-tutor is well weird. He's scared of us, like a cornered rat. But beneath it he's not too bad, he says some OK things, except no-one ever hears 'cos no-one listens. Tracey does; I think Tracey fancies him, she's always lookin' out for him like she's his long-lost granny. This week in form period he has a go at government and Thatcher and how they wrecked the community here. It's unusual for a teacher to say those things but it's right: she killed this community.

I scuffin' hate Thatcher. She and the police made our lives Hell for a year, as well as killing off loads of other families around us. Before 1984, Dad worked in one of the pits, not going down it, in the office. He was proud of that; his dad and most of his family had been down the pit, he worked on top. He supported the miners during the strike.

The Mountain

It was hard for this family, with no money coming in for almost a year. Mum still worked, so we didn't lose the house. She had it rough, working all day, then looking after and feeding the family. Others had it tougher though, with really no money coming in for almost a year.

We lost the strike, we never had a chance of winning it. Afterwards Dad got a job driving a digger for the council, we were proud of him 'cos he bounced back. Eddie used to help him sometimes. Most of the miners we knew were out of work, they either couldn't face trying to learn a new skill or moving away from their families and their roots. But Dad bounced back and we were all proud.

Charon also makes funny quips about this an' that, I think he thinks he's so much cleverer than all of us that no-one except him will get it. We get it, but he doesn't even notice. He probably thinks that because I don't talk I'm thick. Tracey thinks he's cool; he can do no wrong. She's lent him her favourite Smiths' tape, and only arranged to meet him for a drink! I'm like, "Tracey, he's a teacher! What you playin' at?" Tracey's like, "Yeah? So? Don't be so quick to judge people because of what they are. He's interested in us, he's into our music."

"What's that got to do with it?"

"He's comin' to the gig."

"What?"

"He's interested. How often can you say that about anyone in this place, for God's sake? And he'll buy us a drink."

He does, an' all. He only shows up at the Hart on the last Friday of half-term. Becky and I have already done some lighter fuel, I'm dizzy from the buzz and the cider afterwards, now in the Hart we're all wasted, I hardly recognise him when he comes in. Tracey's all excited of course. And he buys us drinks, lots of them. The lads eye him up like he's weird. Emma and Karen and their slaggy friends give him dead eyes, like, 'who do *you* think you are, comin' in *our* pub,' but no-one cares what they think.

The Mountain

And then I think, yeh, Tracey's right, he *is* different, how
many other square teachers would come in here with us?
An' then he goes and spoils it, makes a twat of himself by
pretending to know the Smiths' lyrics, and of course
everyone laughs, an' so he goes, an' that's it. He skulks off
like a thief into the night. So we're on our own again,
getting' wasted, sharin' a table with a load of people I don't
even *like*.

None of this is worth anything. I can get trashed,
but that just numbs me. It makes me sad again.

I can't play tonight; I can't go on. We're due to
start in an hour or so, we're all wasted. Rick can't keep
time at the best of times. Will's playing is really erratic. I
know what they'll say, though, if I say anything. "Oh, go
on, Anna. Do it for Eddie. He would have wanted you to."
The bastards, it's a powerful argument, even though they
don't know how I feel they can still blackmail me like that
and it works.

I have to run out and see to Darren. They give me
a look, the band that is, like "Oh, yeh! You're gonna split
an' not come back." How many of them have got thieving
little bastards for brothers that they have to clothe and
feed? I'm like, "I'll be back for 9, OK?" they're all like,
"yeh, *right.*" But I haven't let them down for a gig before.
I may be a drop-out glue-head who misses school and
disappears for days, but the gig is sacred to me 'cos of
Eddie, and deep down they know that.

The park isn't far away; five minutes' walk
through the mud and rain and I'm back. Some scabby
looking lads from the caravan just down from us are having
a bong and invite me to blow with them. I accept;
sometimes they do stronger stuff, which does my head in.
This is OK. After five to ten minutes my head's buzzin'
again, if I can keep feelin' like this I'll be OK to go on.
Colours, noises, smells are all very intense after a smoke,

although the glue and lighter fuel deaden your senses. I've got such a cocktail inside me that my body's confused.

Darren's in the caravan, playing his Nintendo and watching a video at the same time. I heat up some water and make him a pot-noodle I skanked from the Late Shop near the Hart. I hesitate a bit, then crash him five fags for the evening. I hesitate some more, then leave him the dregs of the bottle of cider from before. He's well made up, and sorted for the evening now. If I hadn't done this, he'd have been out nicking things and knowing my luck would have picked tonight to get himself caught, the little git. With Dad gone walkabout and likely to come home trashed and me at the gig, he'd have spent the night in a cell until we could get him out. However bad he is he don't deserve that, so this is me looking out for him, fixing up the least bad arrangement for his Friday evening. I wrap some bed clothes round his skinny little rat's body, turn on the gas heater which he's too useless to turn on for himself, and give him a big cuddle.

Only trouble is, now I've no booze left. I hate doin' this, but I stand outside the Legion waiting for the dirty old men who're about to go in. I hate this not just 'cos of the dirty old men, but 'cos Dad goes to the legion. He'll be in the Red Lion now, that's for sure, but the men in the Legion all know him. Then again, by the time he gets up there he'll be too wrecked to understand. "Your daughter was trying to cadge drinks off us earlier on this evening. Pretty little thing, if only she'd smile a bit more." He'll understand tomorrow, all right, when he goes in after our spring cleaning game, an' then I'm dead. But tomorrow's another time, this is now, and I need a drink.

"Hey, mister, here's a fiver. Get us a small bottle of vodka."

"Ey, up! It's Arthur Lomas' girl!"

"Ey, up, Anna. Remember when you used to sit on my knee, when you were that little!"

65

The Mountain

"She'll sit on your knee tonight, an' all! Get her a bottle, an' she'll sit on all us knees!"

"Ey, up! Fancy sittin' on us knees, Anna?"

"What would Arthur say, if he knew you was scroungin' drinks off old men?"

"He'd be too pissed! If he weren't, he'd sit her on his own knee!"

I hate this; I hate them. I'd like to stab them all in the eyes, the dirty old bastards. But they can get me my drink, so I try real hard and force a watery smile. A particularly filthy lookin' old git presses his grotty hand longer than is necessary into mine and takes my fiver. He comes out ten minutes later, if anything looking like more of an old wreck than he did before he went in, and comes right up to me, breathing his filthy tobacco and whisky flavoured stench of a breath all over me. He puts his rank sweaty arms round me.

"Here you are my sweetheart. Now you be a good girl, see? Now what about a kiss for your old uncle Ernest?"

"Fuck off, you stinkin' old coffin-dodger," I tell him, and I run off with my hard-earned bottle.

I'm in the woods across from the Hart and the leisure centre now. I take a couple of big swigs from the bottle. I have a little bit of blow left on me and I roll up a smoke. I'm wet through, half-covered in mud and numb with booze, lighter fuel and blow. I look at my watch: 8.45. We're on in fifteen minutes.

I don't care if we're on. I sit down among some leaves and finish my smoke, plus a few more swigs. I look up at the outline of the crazy trees against the black night sky. The moon is just coming out of a cloud. Through the trees I can see the outline of Mam Nick and Mam Tor, the shivering mountain. I couldn't say I was exactly comfortable out here – I'm cold and hungry for a start – but I feel OK. They're all inside the bar, I'm pretty sure, and

66

here I can be by myself, don't need to get looked at by no-one and don't need to talk to no-one. I like it like that.

I'm losin' track of time but after a while I decide I'd
better find the others. I go into the pub but they've
left, just a few old crusties playin' dominoes or something.
Someone's puked up on the floor and it's just been left –
the place stinks. I make for the leisure centre. Some knob
on the door doesn't want to let me in at first, but I tell him
I'm with the band. He still won't budge, so I have to send
for Will, who thinks he's the band leader. He pushes me in
then drags me backstage.

"Where the hell have you been? It's 9:30!"

"So? We've done the sound check – never heard of a
band being late?"

"The others are goin' mental! We're ready to start."

"Just give me two minutes. Loo."

"Come *on!*"

"Ladies' prerogative. Powdering my nose and suchlike."

I go into the loo, have a last little smoke, finish the vodka
bottle and feel all dizzy. My head is spinning, there are
devils in my head, and I'm sweating like a pig even though
it's freezing in this dump. I lean over a sink and puke my
guts up.

I feel dead but force myself through the door. There
are hundreds of people in the main hall and it spooks me a
bit. Through the haze I see the distant shape of my crazy
form tutor, Charon. *What's he doin'?* I thought he'd
learned his lesson and buggered off for good, back to his
snotty poncey quiche-eating friends. What the hell does he
want in a dump like this? I try my best to hide but he's
clocked me. He's heading towards me, only his path is

67

The Mountain

blocked by about a hundred people. He's got something in
his hand. What will happen first, will he, Mr Polite, fight
his way through a hundred sweaty moshers, punks and
skinheads, or will I, with my madly spinning head and my
blurred vision, make it to the safety of the dressing room?
It's gonna be close, but somehow he makes it through the
throngs of bodies and is standing a few feet away from me.

"Anna," he calls out.

The sea of bodies between us won't part; he's not
gonna

make it. He reaches this brown paper bag towards
me.

"Here". I open it. It's two cans of Heineken. I
feel

really sick.

"Good luck with the gig."

I look at him. His big blue eyes are like an
innocent

puppy's. He's right, he don't belong in here.

"Thanks," I goes.

Chapter 7

I'm humiliated; I should never have come.

When I was studying, I read a play in which a middle-class guy tries to be all working - class. He wants to fit in, he wants to join this band of terrorists who are fighting the very ideals and values he personifies. They don't accept him; while it is possible for a member of the working classes to embourgeois himself, to aspire to and then join the middle-classes – indeed it is the blueprint for many a self-made man in our dog-eat-dog, market forces - driven society – the reverse can never happen. You are always found out, it is as if you have engraved on your forehead the words 'Caution! Middle–class, educated Volvo driver trying to pass himself as working-class!' The author, of course, put it more plainly. "C'est une question de peau" his would-be working-class terrorist is told. No matter what act you commit, no matter how hard you try or how earnestly you mean it, you can't make that transition. You can't fit in, you'll be found out immediately. It's a matter of your skin, and you can't change your skin.

My skin wasn't the right kind for that pub.

I leave, humiliated. What was I thinking of going there in the first place? The Swan is no longer an option. I can't face people right now, especially the nosy sort who will ask questions, still less the 'I told you so' sort who will gloat at being right. There is a rough-looking off-licence nearby. I go in and buy a small bottle of vodka and a four-pack of Heineken. I walk around the edge of the dark, menacing woods on the edge of town and drain the vodka bottle. The Heinekens are my insurance for later on. I think of food, I am cold and hungry, and I think of cooking in my flat.

I was back in France. There was a quiet menace in the air. I met Marcia a few days later. She had a black eye. Her lip was swollen to about twice its normal size. I was so stunned, I wanted to cry. How could anyone do this? How could anything matter so much that they did this? I asked her if Paolo was angry. She said nothing, took off her blouse. "À tel point que.." she began, but the sentence did not need to be finished. She had a red, angry scar below her belly-button, running in the shape of a smile from one hip-bone to the other. The stitches were still in place; the scar was very tender and very fresh.

Gianluca her brother called round to see us later on that evening. He knew; nothing remained a secret for any length of time amongst these mountains. They passed on secrets but they guarded them jealously from the outside world, from the foreigners in the next valley with their different ways and different patois. But no-one kept a secret within the valley; the mountains kept them to themselves.

Gianluca wanted revenge; it was the Italian way, the family way. I was family; Paolo no longer was. Paolo was disowned, disinherited. I was family, so this wasn't my fault. Gianluca wanted me to know that; like Paolo, he wasn't angry with me. He had sworn revenge, and those dark moody mountains would already have passed the message on to Paolo.

About an hour passes and, after the vodka, things begin to take on a different complexion, even if I can not. I will go to the gig. I will stick out like a sore thumb, I will be laughed at behind my back, but I will go. This evening has worked out so badly, I have nothing else to lose. I will go late, but I will go.

The leisure centre is the dreadful, sardine-packed dive I expected it to be. After the décor in the Hart, I am at least prepared. The faded yellow paintwork and the nicotine-stained ceiling match in an unplanned sort of way. It is too hot and incredibly noisy. There is a bar which it is impossible to get near, so I am at least relieved that I stocked up internally beforehand. And then, across a crowded room, I see Anna.

She should be onstage by now, but of course they too are late. I try to move towards her, but it is a battle against an enormous tide of youths dancing, swaying, gyrating in every possible direction. But then, a minor miracle happens. The sea of sweaty youths before me parts, and Moses-like I am able to stand in the gap and capitalise. If anything, I am being pushed towards Anna.

I am standing yards away from her; she looks dreadful. I hand her the two cans of Heineken.

"Thanks," she says. As simply as that. Like she's never not spoken.

Even in my numbed state, I am blown away by this. I am as awake, all of a sudden, as if I had been slapped in the face. She has spoken. After two months, she has done to me what she will do to no other member of staff, to no other person, virtually. She has exchanged a word.

The gig is OK. They start with some very fast and noisy numbers. Three of the band flay around making an unnecessary amount of noise and fuss. My attention, however, is focused entirely on the waif-like, enigmatic figure at the back of the stage. Anna lurks blackly, half hidden behind a bass guitar nearly as big as herself. She appears to be playing for no-one. She is completely impervious to the audience and to the others in the band. I

71

get the feeling she is doing this only for herself, and there is something about that that appeals to me. Her long black skirt and hooded top give the impression of a member of some secretive religious sect. One of my cans of Heineken are on stage beside her, balanced precariously on an amp.

Four or five very noisy songs follow each other with unremitting aggression. I find it difficult to understand how four such little people are capable of making all that noise. Then things quieten down slightly for a while, the guitarist goes acoustic and plays some bearable songs, although I still can't hear the words. After about an hour, the singer announces that this is their last song. I hear something about lights going out, then they come on. My head is buzzing from the noise and the electricity, but I made it. I survived their gig.

A gangly youth with a backwards baseball cap informs us through a very muffled microphone that there will be a short break, then the main band will be on. I still have two beers and a burning desire for some fresh air. I've done my bit for the evening, and I am confident the next band can triumph without my presence in the arena. Behind the leisure centre there is an attempt at a little garden. I wander amongst the trees and bushes, relieved to be alone after having been in such close proximity to so many people. As I open my can I am aware of a noise at the far corner of the little garden. A dark figure hunches forward, I think, then I see the tell-tale glimmer of a burning cigarette end through the mist.

The figure lurches towards me. It is Anna.

"What did you think?"

"Anna?" I'm still finding it difficult to come to terms with her talking. For all I know she has said more to me tonight than she has to anyone all year.

"What did you think? It's important to me."

"Me? I hardly think that what *I* think is important to anyone. And you don't strike me as being the type to care too much what people think anyway." Why am I

72

being like this? She has broken the habit of the last two years and spoken, and I'm being a pompous teacher.

"Well you're wrong." She sounds annoyed. If I could stand back a bit and be an objective observer, I wouldn't blame her. "I care a lot. I need to know what you thought."

I look into her face and it is momentarily illuminated by the sudden appearance of moonlight. Her eyes are pleading, her white skin is so thin I can almost make out the veins beneath it. She looks impossibly frail.

I swallow. "Well, I didn't like the noisy stuff. The acoustic stuff was OK. I liked that last song, the one about the lights going out. But they came on."

She smiles. Even looking dog-rough and tired as she does, she has something unmistakeably attractive about her. I have hardly ever seen her smile, nor can I imagine that many people have. It is indescribably wonderful and beautiful. It is uncomplicated, uncompromised, and real.

"That'll do for me."

Nothing prepares me for what happens next.

She comes right up to me, throws her fag on the ground, puts both her hands on my shoulders, and kisses me on the lips. She smiles, takes a sip of my lager, and kisses me again. I'm in a state of shock. I manage to emit some noise, a sort of strangled grunt.

"Sssh." She still has her arms around me, and wants to continue kissing. I'm losing, so I decide to give in. So I kiss her back. I close my eyes and am lost, I am dizzy, yet this moment is so fragile I fear losing it. If I open my eyes I will awaken from a sweet dream and there is no going back to it. I try to concentrate; nothing around us is real, only this.

I try to pull myself together. This really is not happening. She stops, then I stop. Curiously, for people who have just decided to talk to each other for the only time in two months, we have nothing to say. She takes a swig from my beer. We share another one. The night is cold; she only wears a denim jacket over her black garb for warmth. Protectively, I put my arm around her, and for a brief moment she rests her head on my shoulder, as if she could sleep. I really feel that she could sleep. I want to keep the tenderness of this vulnerable moment, I want to keep it for ever.

Anna pulls away from me quite abruptly, then leaves as suddenly as she approached me in the first place, and with as little warning. I'm still stunned. By the time I come to my senses I am alone in this little garden.

I rush round to the front of the leisure centre. Rebecca is on the front steps, draped around some pimply youth, the ubiquitous cider bottle in hand.

"Ey up, *Nigel.* Like the music?"

"Yes, er, well, it's OK. Look this is important, have you seen Anna?"

"*Anna?*"

"Yes, trust me it's really important, I've got to speak with her."

"You'll have a job."

"Yes, I know, I mean, oh God! Look, she's lost something, a bracelet I think, I-"

"Well, give it me."

"What?"

"Give it me."

I half want to say "give it *to* me", but perhaps not now. "This is really urgent. I must see her."

"She's got that many bracelets, another one more or less won't matter."

She'll be with t'band." This is the pimply youth, who is obviously getting tired of the exchange, perhaps as it is eating into his snogging time, or cider drinking time.

"And they'll be..?"

"Dunno. Sometimes they go back to Will's or Rick's."

"Which is where?" I want to shake him.

The Mountain

"Dunno." For a minute he does an almost passable impression of someone thinking. "They might have headed down the hill. Unless they've gone in to see the second band."

Now I want to kiss him, but instead head for the hill going down into town at a speed my body has not moved at since I was about fourteen. A long way ahead, perhaps half a mile, a group of youths walk unsteadily, spilling onto the road. I change up a gear and head for them.

The rain is lashing against my face. Moments ago, in the garden, I didn't even notice it. Now it's as if it's never been away. I'm running in the middle of the road, running down the pot-holed road, almost completely out of control. My body aches, it is crying out for mercy, but I not only keep going, I don't think I could stop if I had to.

Now I am almost alongside them. A gaunt, sombre figure brings up the rear. She walks alone, taking no part in the noisy, animated discussion ahead of her. My heart misses a beat, as this has to be Anna. In a manoeuvre of which the SAS would be proud, I stealthily grab hold of her jacket and attract her attention without anyone else in the group noticing. I pull her to one side.

"Anna," I whisper urgently. "We've got to talk."

She smiles, no doubt amused by the idea.

We skulk in the shadow of a hedge, then make for an empty 'phone booth. We are so close we can smell each other's breath. We try to talk. We don't talk. We kiss again, briefly. Outside on the pavement another group of youths walk by, then the odd straggler or two. It seems as if half the town is picking this very moment to walk past this very 'phone booth. Plainly making last orders in town has proved a more attractive option to some than hearing the complete set of the last band.

"Anna," I say.

The Mountain

"Sssh," she replies, in an uncanny echo of part of our exchange in the leisure centre garden. We kiss once more. My body, which was so numb not long ago, is buzzing; I have pins and needles all over. My stomach feels hollow, empty, it trembles. I feel sick with so much feeling all at once.

"What happens now?" I don't even understand my own question. Do I mean, *now* now, or a more serious, important kind of now?

"You can come with us now…" I don't think she means the same now as I do, though. As her voice trails off, I understand that she thinks that her suggestion is a bad idea.

"I don't think so."

"I wish you could stay. I wish we could stay together."

"Me too." But I think I am thinking longer term than she is.

"It's impossible."

"I know."

"It's a mess."

"I know." I just want to hold her, for ever. She is so incredibly frail, she needs someone, and this frailty is strangely beautiful.

"It can't work. Nothing can ever work."

"I know." I wish I could say something else. I wish I could say things I don't mean. I simply can't sound insincere. It must sound terrible, I must be saying the kind of things she doesn't want and doesn't *need* to hear, but I can't say what I don't feel. And this can't work. It is like a beautiful dream at the moment, but it can't work. Her beauty is too delicate, too frail.

"Come with us. We're going to Will's."

"You know that can't work. Can I see you tomorrow?"

"That can't work."

"Sunday?"

The Mountain

She looks at me in a strange way.

The group are at the bottom of the hill now. A couple of youths are calling her name. Someone is walking back up the hill towards us. Some drunks across the road are singing. Anna tries to leave the 'phone booth to join her party, but I hold her back. Even that little gesture can't work. She opens the door and I know I am not going with her. I know that we will never relive this moment, and that hurts.

"My whole life is like a Sunday," she says.

Chapter 8

We're on fire tonight. We rock. From the moment that the initial feedback is let loose, then the introductory drum solo, then the crashing guitars, I know that *The Queen is Dead* is going to be just right. The drumming sounds perfect, and Will's guitar playing is spot on this time. Again we're in G. The intro comes crashing through: G flat, C, G sharp minor, B minor, and then that first verse with lots of D, then shifting to F, then G. Only I'm behind, they're playing too fast. I really hammer out the last four chords on the G and the C at the end of the bars. I spend the entire song trying to catch up, but after three and a half minutes I'm half a beat behind the others, just like I was at the beginning. But we're satisfied; we can't believe we sound this good after the mess of a rehearsal the other week. We rock; everyone loves *Hand in Glove, Ask, Panic, I Started Something*, and 'specially *Sweet and Tender Hooligan*. I'm nervous when the songs get quieter – you can hear our mistakes more. But Will's acoustic guitar on *The Boy With the Thorn in his Side, Half a Person* and *Girlfriend in a Coma* is really sensitive, he's really improved a lot. When it comes to *There is a Light* we're all playing our best, just like rehearsal the other week. The bass plays itself. I like playing bass 'cos you can skulk in the background, all in black, and no-one need know you're there. But they'd know if you're not there, you hold the songs together. It's an OK arrangement to me.

I can't believe it's gone so well; I can't believe it's gone at all. We're all so wasted, especially me, it's a

wonder we could even stand up and hold our instruments.
And I've enjoyed it. We did it properly, we did it for
Eddie, and we actually enjoyed it. We rocked.

I feel really strange afterwards, a bit like coming
down on valium. It felt so great, now there's nothing
where there was a rush and noise. I go outside for a smoke.
I'm not bothered about the other band. I'll have a smoke,
perhaps a little drink to bring me down, then we'll go back
to Wills and party a bit. I'll still be home before Dad, and
in better nick.

I mix up my smoke in the skanky little garden
they have in back of the leisure centre. I don't want to be
seen, for quite a few reasons, actually, so I try to blend in
with the trees. There are worse things to blend in with.
But there's a noise. Just for a moment, I am terrified, I can
hear but I can't see. Then this shape moves out of the
gloom, and it's strangely recognisable. I wouldn't have
believed it, but it's Charon.

I don't want to be seen. I've half a joint in my
hand but I'm not gonna waste it, I just hope he's cool
enough not to bust me or dozy enough not to notice. I can't
hide here, so I walk towards him. I goes, "What did you
think?" It's a lame question, I know, but I can't get my
head round talkin' to him just yet. He's like, "Anna?", like
he's seen a ghost. I must look a bit like a ghost, a black
ghost, but he looks pretty rough himself. I goes, "What did
you think? It's important to me." Why am I talking like
this? Is it really important to me what he thinks? Tonight I
do actually care whether we were good or not, but that isn't
the same as caring about what people think. I *know* we
were good. Then he starts goin' all teacher-like on me, all
pompous and talking down to me, like he's tryin' to score
points, an' all I'm tryin' to do, for once, is talk to the guy.
He goes, "Well I hardly think that what I think is important
to anyone," and some other lame stuff about wondering
whether I care what he thinks, and I really don't need this.
"You're wrong," I goes, and he is. He may have all the

79

education and the rest but he doesn't understand naff all about me. And I don't know why, but I am really disappointed. "I care a lot. I need to know what you thought."

Now I can see his face in the pale moonlight. My God I thought I looked bad. He looks like a ghost. He's still in teacher-mode - "Well, I didn't like the noisy stuff. The acoustic stuff was OK. I liked that last song, the one about the lights going out." But that last bit really touches me; it means a lot, 'cos that's the song that means everything to me. It's pathetic, but in those few words he's undone all the bad things he said before, and I want to kiss him. This feels very special.

I swear to God this is true. I black out for a minute. I go all dizzy and faint, I see colours rushing through my head and I see white light, the waves of the ocean are crashing inside my head, and then I hear a loud ringing noise. And I look up and, I swear to God I don't know why or how, but I kiss him, he kisses me, it's like we're never going to stop. And then he wants to tell me something and all I can say is "Sssh." My arms are wrapped around him and I feel safe. I close my eyes and am lost, I am dizzy and I don't really know if this is real, any of it, but I feel safe, I feel like someone cares. Now I realise this is the only time since Eddie I've ever felt like this. Apart from Eddie, no-one has ever made me feel that they really cared.

It's all too much for me, this is; I can't cope. It's like I've had nearly two years of being a walking zombie, then all of a sudden there's all this emotion come from nowhere. The last two years my feelings have been dead, now everything is alive again and it's real. But is it real? Or is it my dead feelings that are real?

I'm confused and scared and maybe a little paranoid, that happens, so I do probably the last thing I should do in this situation: I run. Not, like, a massive run out on the tops, but I run away from this. I run out of the garden and meet up with Rick and Will and the others, and I'm gone.

I'm walking behind them down Old Manchester Hill, about half a mile, when Charon only pops up beside me. He's like, "Anna, we've got to talk." Nobody else calls me by my name. My mates take it for granted that I know they're talking to me; Dad and Darren take me for granted so much they hardly talk to me, except 'what's for tea?' Teachers think I'm scum not worth bothering with. And this one calls me by my name, I've hardly ever heard it before; it sounds quite nice. So I smile; yes, it sounds pretty.

He must know this is well dodgy, chasin' me all the way down a main road. Snogging in the leisure centre garden is one thing, I don't think that would qualify him for a teacher of the year award, but this…So we hide in the shadow of a hedge, then make for an empty 'phone booth. We try to talk some more, but kiss instead. Half of the world is walkin' by outside, we don't care. And I think, let them stare.

I goes, "You can come with us," but that's not gonna happen. He's out of place with us, he's sweet with me now but he'd be no use in a crowd. It's best no-one else sees us. And I'm worried, 'cos I think they have seen us, and that just adds to the sick feeling inside my stomach, the one next to the hollow feeling caused by shock that someone cares about me. It's an OK feeling, I quite like it, I don't want it to go away 'cos it means I'm not dead inside. It's just that it makes me feel sick.

"I don't think so," he goes.

"I wish you could stay. I wish we could stay together."

"Me too."

"It's impossible."

"I know."

"It's a mess."

The Mountain

"I know." Is that all he can say? I need a bit more than that: 'I know'. I feel really helpless.

"It can't work," I goes. "Nothing can ever work."

"I know." I wish he could say something else. But in spite of that, he asks, "Can I see you tomorrow?"

"That can't work."

"Sunday?"

He has no idea how I live. He knows nothing about my life. I wish I could tell him and let him know how I hate Sunday, I'm scared of Sunday, and I really do mean scared; I dread it. But I can't, the words don't come out. I have dried up and in a minute he'll be gone. This will probably never happen again. And I feel very sad.

Will an' that are yellin' at me now. A couple of youths are calling me name. I try to leave, he wants to stop me, but that won't work either. This won't happen again and I'm scared of everything – school, my mates, the dark, the trees, The Park, the caravan, Dad, Darren, everything I have to do to keep us going, my memories that keep me awake at night, and the weekend, especially Sunday.

I join my mates and I feel empty. It's not love that I want, it's certainly not a boyfriend – I've never gone with anyone. At school everyone either treats me like scum or they *are* scum. And it's definitely nothing to do with sex. I don't need that at all. Sex as far as I can see has nothing to do with feelings, it's brute movement, it's sore and ugly, and it's dirty old men leering. I don't know much but I know it's nothing for me. Tonight was well different. It *felt* good; it felt right and it felt real. He was there for me, he was lookin' out for me, he held me when I was cold. That's a million miles away from the dirty old sods who wait around outside the legion or the leisure centre ogling the girls in their stupid little uniforms. I don't want no sex, I don't need that. But I want someone to care enough to hold me tight when I'm scared and cold.

We go back to Will's. It should be good, but I feel flat. We smoke a bit more, drink a bit more, but I'm not in the mood. I feel really empty. Charon has gone, I don't think he'll be back, not as I saw him today. I should feel good that our gig was good, and good that someone cares a bit about me. Will's like, "Eh, up what's up? Why the long face?" That's his kind of caring, and that's OK, but I can't explain to him how I feel, and no-one else is bothered.

I don't really want to stay long. By the time we have a couple of drinks and a couple of smokes, I'm beginning to feel better, well, less *on edge,* but by then it's midnight and I'd better be going. Just in *case,* in the very unlikely event that Dad gets home not too late. I wanna be there when he gets in.

I walk up that long grey hill that I've walked up so many times before, this time with my face into the wind and rain which not long ago were pelting my back. The strange thing is, I really don't know how I feel tonight. I feel warm inside but I have a stomach-ache, and at the same time I'm a bit numbed, possibly because of all I've had to smoke and drink an' that. I'm still tense and a bit on edge, and my head is spinning with too many different thoughts.

I suddenly feel very lonely now. My mates are still partying. Charon's God knows where, I don't know if I'll ever see him again. Worst of all, it's still half-term now, no escape. Dad'll already have a bag on about me scrounging drinks outside the Legion, *his* Legion, and I've got his company to look forward to, off and on, for a whole week. Tomorrow won't be much fun, the days more or less stumble after each other after that. Then it's back to school. I don't have much to look forward to.

Eddie would have known how I felt; he would have understood. I don't exactly know this; I just think it. He was the only one who ever wondered how I felt, who ever tried to understand. For a start, he was the only one who ever asked. He looked out for me; he looked out for me at school, he was there when people called me a weird

83

The Mountain

freak and when teachers wouldn't give me a chance. God knows what he would have made of the mess I'm in now. But I know one thing: he and I would have had a laugh about it. There aren't too many laughs in my life these days.

As I approach The Moss Park I suddenly feel cold and hungry. I climb the long muddy bank up to our caravan near the top, and then my heart sinks and my stomach seems to drop, feeling even more hollow and even more sick. There's a light on in the caravan.

I can't believe the devastation inside. My first thought is, we've been robbed. We've been done over. Dad's lying on the middle of the floor, half undressed, his face is badly swollen like he's hit it against something. There's blood around his hair and ear, although that's not so unusual. What is unusual, and really spooks me, is the expression on his face; he looks in agony, like he's been crying, or howling, or just really afraid an' lonely, but there was no-one there. His face is frozen in pain and fear, like he saw himself about to be attacked, he saw his fate runnin' towards him and couldn't do nothin' about it.

He looks positively good compared to Darren. Darren's lyin' half in, half out of bed. His face is one swollen bruise, and it's already gone purple. Snot, blood and saliva are crusted around his mouth which is sort of half-open, like a fish that's just been caught. There are red scratches all down both arms, I can see 'cos his shirts been ripped. As he breathes he whimpers asthmatically, like a little puppy with a sore paw. He's lost two teeth, and his mouth is bloody.

There's furniture all over the place, it seems weird to worry about furniture at a time like this, but I can't help noticing it. Two chairs have been thrown, by the looks of things, and now lie on the floor. Our other bedside lamp has been smashed. The table's been pushed right into one corner, and for some reason water's running from the tap.

84

The Mountain

The floor's covered in mud and water, nearly as much as there is outside.

It's hard to describe how I feel; and I was confused enough *before* this. Now I'm spooked. I try to gather my thoughts. To think about where to begin with this whole sorry mess, I know one thing above all that really freaks me – I'll probably never know exactly what happened in here. Dad'll have been too wasted, that's for sure, and Darren'll be too petrified, either of Dad or of whoever else it was.

We've been attacked before – just after we moved in. Anyone can force this door open, Darren could. I walked in late one Sunday morning, I'd been out running, and I found Dad starin' at a flick-knife, Darren huddled in fear in a corner. Gangs come in from the city at the weekend, do the rounds of the caravans and nick what little there is to sell on; they know that these places don't lock and the people who live in them won't go to the police. But this wasn't a gang. This was a couple of local thugs who'd come to offer Dad 'protection', Mafia style. Dad didn't want it so they threatened to cut Darren up a bit, just to make a point. They were makin' their point to Dad when I came in. I'll never forget the look of humiliation on his face.

So we pay them; Dad pays them each month, what little he has left after he's boozed an' gambled it away. They look out for us against the gangs, so they reckon, they keep the police off The Park (they wouldn't come around here anyway) and they control the drugs on The Park. If you don't pay, they do your place over, just to flex their muscles a bit. That's what they were doin' this first time: flexin' their muscles a bit.

So what's happened tonight? My blood runs cold as I try and piece it together. What scares me to death is, was Darren here by himself when they broke in? Where were the people who're supposed to be lookin' out for him? Getting' wrecked and getting' stoned, while he was frightened for his life. We don't exactly have much to do, Darren doesn't demand much, just that we look out for him a bit. He's eight and we failed him big time.

Or, was Dad in? Did they follow him home as he staggered and stumbled up the slope – easy pickings from a wrecked old tramp who lives in a caravan? Did Darren wake up to his screams as he got thrown to the floor, smacked around by his own furniture, cowering in fear as his own Dad's too wrecked, too weak and defenceless to know where he is as he falls to the floor time after time? Where's his big sister, the one who says she'll look out for him?

The third possibility scares me more than the other two put together. Did Dad do this? He's hit us before. He's bound to be in a foul mood after hearing about me outside the Legion. He'll have been the laughing stock of his drinking mates, because of his daughter. Should I have got the beating that Darren got – were those bruises meant for me? When Dad's *really* wrecked, he's capable of almost anything, if he can stand up, that is. Did he come home so wrecked, and so angry, he wanted to hit his own family? Did he come home that trashed, but not so trashed he was unable to stand? And what really gets me is, I'll never know; he won't remember.

I roll Dad over, wipe down his face and hair, and put him on his side so he don't choke. I can't lift him so I just chuck his bed clothes over him, arranging them as carefully as I can so as not to wake him and to give him maximum warmth. I take a cold cloth to Darren to try and soothe his swollen face and I wipe the blood from around his face. He's shivering. I climb into bed with him, put my arms around his broken little body. In a while he'll be warmer, with the warmth from my body. I feel confused and strange. I breathe over him, as if I could breathe life into him, like I wished I could when I first saw Eddie's dead, broken body. I've got to keep him warm. I cradle him in my arms, and as I try to drift off to sleep I hear

86

The Mountain

someone crying, broken little sobs at first, then longer and louder. Quite a while passes before I realise it is me. I should have been here for him.

Chapter 9

"People saw you!" Tracey is incredulous. Anna is silent. I sweat and remain silent too.

It's the first Monday back after half-term, I should be free but I'm on cover for the first half-lesson – Art (just my luck as you can't do any of your own work; it takes twenty minutes each to set up and pack away and pupils are always coming up to you asking how to draw someone running) and 5th year (just my luck because it includes some of the people I really don't want to see at all, sundry do-gooders and assorted malevolent gossips all gathered within the same four walls). I am tired and I just want to switch off and sleep.

"Are you listening to me?!"

"Tracey, I…"

"Well?"

I sigh. This isn't working.

"Yes, of course I'm listening to you. With you pressed up against my desk so closely I scarcely have any option."

Tracey, I think, is one of those pupils who must sit at the very front in every lesson she has. Anna seems to, too, for some reason. In this particular case, a very overcrowded Art room, the claustrophobic effect is accentuated and it is as if she is sitting on top of me.

"What was you both thinking about?" I don't have the energy to correct her – not that she is giving me the opportunity. She continues without drawing breath:

"Hundreds of people saw you. In a 'phone booth!

The Mountain

We saw you, for God's sake, on our way back home. And if *we* saw you, who's to say that everyone else didn't?"

I find this logic difficult to counter, but I make a weak attempt.

"Oh, come *on,* you can't be sure about-"

"Don't you tell me what I am and aren't sure about!" and although I'm still not convinced by the grammar, she sounds like someone twenty years her senior - twenty years *my* senior. I fully expect a slap in the face at any minute.

"Tracey-"

"Don't you 'Tracey' *me,*" she counters, a little unreasonably I feel. "The fact is, you was both well out of order. You've both been well irresponsible and not thought about the consequences. Now who's going to pick up the pieccs?"

I feel like a murderer, or a war-criminal. Anna looks up at me wretchedly. Tracey's haranguing is for the benefit of both of us.

Two tables behind Tracey sit a group of girls taking very animatedly. I vaguely recognise a few of them. They keep looking up at Tracey and Anna, and at me, which I find more than disconcerting. Then one of them approaches my desk.

"Excuse me, *sir,*" she says in what I fancy is a nasty tone of voice. "I can't quite seem to get the lips right, can you help?"

"What?"

"The *lips,*" she repeats, with more emphasis than I like. "How do I make them, you know, pout?"

"I'm sorry, I really haven't got a clue," I answer honestly.

"Oh, OK," she replies evenly. Halfway between my desk and hers, she says something that sounds a bit like "he says he's not an expert with lips". The pupils at her table laugh savagely.

"I'm surprised," I hear one say.

89

The Mountain

"Well, I'm only going on what he said. I didn't ask for a practical demonstration."

The entire table collapses with laughter.

"Sssh," I entreat weakly.

"Oh, sorry, *sir,*" replies a voice dripping in sarcasm.

"*See!!*" Tracey whispers to me with considerably more force, and this time I really do expect her to hit me. "*They* know. What more proof d'you want? And they hate us. They hate Anna."

"Well that's hardly something for which I can be blamed."

"Don't be so irrelevant! They'd do anything to get at Anna. They can't stand her. They hate the way she gets special treatment, gets away with not talking, they're jealous of the attention she gets in the band, jealous of the lads…"

"Weren't some of them in the pub before the gig? Didn't I buy them a drink?"

Tracey looks incredulous. "You can't *buy* any of us. You can't make us *like* you, by buying us drinks. They hate Anna, which means they now hate you, just like they also hate me. They're out to get us. They were only in the pub to get some lads – my boyfriend John, Becky's brother – anything to upset us. They only go to the gig to see the band fail, so they can laugh if it does."

"Who are they?"

"The two in the pub were Emma Beswick and Karen Hurst. You teach Emma, in case you hadn't noticed. She's hated you right from the start, says you ignore her. Karen, her mate's the one who just came up to your desk. She's always picking on Anna. They'll do anything to spoil her life. The others are their mates, so they do what they do."

The remainder of the cover lesson passes without incident. I am relieved when the half-bell goes and I can go. The door opens and Judy Hartington walks in. The

The Mountain

background hum of conversation disappears at once.
Tracey coughs and cranes forward so I can hear her.

"This is all we need."

"I'm sorry, Tracey, this time you really have lost me."

"That old bag Hartington," she spits impatiently. "She's nosey as hell, always listening to the pupils' problems, you know, like 'you can tell *me,* you know, girls. I'm here to help, I'm here to listen'. She a nosey old bag and a right gossip. As soon as you go, that lot'll be up at the desk bending her ear."

"Just like you have until now, in fact." But my answer can't conceal the fact that I'm scared.

Judy casts me a frosty look as we swap positions.

"Good morning, Mr Charon. Did you have an agreeable half-term break?"

"Oh, yes thanks Mrs Hartington. And you?"

"Ms," she corrects me. "Oh,gid thanks. Mostly uneventful."

We stand for a moment, without quite knowing what to say to each other.

"How was the 'gig'?"

"Oh…" I can't think how to describe it.

"Eventful," I hear Tracey mutter under her breath.

It is barely 10 o'clock as I enter the staffroom, and already I am stunned by this morning's events. To live through so much this early in the morning is not useful after a week of long lie-ins.

The strange thing is, I remember very little about the night of the gig. I had drunk more by the time it began than I do in an average week. I remember giving Anna her cans of Heineken, I can remember she spoke. I can remember being with her in the garden, I can remember drinking some more. I can remember running down a hill after her, in the rain.

91

The Mountain

Small snippets of the jigsaw are trying to come back to me, as indeed they have been all week. What did we talk about? What is so wrong about us talking? What were we doing in a 'phone booth? Something more than just talking, although that much has only really become clear to me today, largely through Tracey's admonishments. What on earth can have happened? And why do I feel so uneasy?

Anthony breezes into the staffroom, full of the joys of autumn, and interrupts my rêverie.

"Now then, Nigel!" he emanates bonhomie. "Good half-term?"

He takes a long look out of the staffroom window, sighs deeply as if he is about to solve one of the great unanswered problems of the age, and says after a long pause:

"Nice weather for ducks!"

He beams with pride at his 'bons mots', as if he single-handedly were responsible for this phrase's introduction into the language and subsequent usage as we know it today.

"Yes, Anthony," I say wearily.

"Oh, well," he says, looking at his watch importantly, "Up an' at 'em."

I think that these are some of the people who like me:

Tracey Spencer. She is a friend of Anna's also in my form. She frets about me like a mother hen, sits right under my nose and provides me with what she must think of as a teacher's emergency survival kit – register? Pen? Red pen? Board rubber? Tracey's here.

Rebecca Woods. I teach her German. She sits at the front near Anna. She chats a lot, she is nearly as talkative as Anna is not, but she seems good-natured. She helps Anna with her work. She is the only pupil apart from Tracey that I have ever heard Anna talk to.

Anna. I think. I hope.

92

The Mountain

I know that these are some of the people who don't like me:

Emma Beswick. I teach her too. She is in a little gang who don't like Anna and who give her a hard time. She gives me a hard time.

Karen Hurst. She is a friend of Emma's which makes her an enemy of Anna. I don't teach her but I don't like the way she looks. She has short ratty blond hair, glasses, and small narrow eyes like a pig's. I don't trust her.

Judy Hartington. I'm not quite sure, but I don't like the way she looks at me. I don't trust her, either.

I have a chance for a quick chat with Tracey after afternoon registration. Anna's there, too, although she's behaving as if she's never seen me before in her life.

"Perhaps," I begin, "we can talk now without being overheard. You've got me quite worried."

"*You're* worried?" Tracey does incredulous very well. "Those bitches Emma and Karen spent the whole second half of the lesson round Hartington's desk. I tried my hardest to hear but couldn't. But from the dead eyes we was getting off them, I know they were telling her everything. *Everything.*"

I'm still quite a bit more confused than I care to let on. Some vital details are missing before my jigsaw puzzle takes on any shape.

"But…will she believe them?"

"Well, you've got to hope that she doesn't. So does Anna." I'd almost forgotten about Anna.

"And…what did they say they'd...seen?"

"I told you, I couldn't hear it all. But Hartington will have got every last detail out of them, you wait. You're in deep shit."

"But…what exactly could they have seen?"

Tracey decides that it is at this moment that she should add sarcasm to her arsenal.

93

The Mountain

"Oh, well, nothing. Nothing very out of the ordinary. Just a form tutor getting a girl in his form pissed, then snogging her, then running after her and snogging her again just in case no-one saw first time round. In a *'phone booth*," she adds at the end, as if it is this last detail that makes the whole thing so reprehensible.

I'm stunned again; this afternoon is starting out worse than this morning did.

"But..." I stammer. I'm searching desperately for appropriate words, and I am sure Tracey sees the irony in this: the pedantic, nit-picking grammar-bore of a teacher momentarily lost for words.

"What's the matter, had you forgotten?"

I dare not tell her the truth – that I had never fully remembered.

"But you told me to buy her a drink!"

This is as weak an answer as I've given at any stage in this whole, sorry saga. The look on Tracey's face tells me that it is beneath her contempt. So, for the moment, am I. They walk out.

I am finding this all very difficult to come to terms with and my stomach is tied in several knots. It is all the worse for the fact that the full realisation of what I have done is only now sinking in; to have been put in the picture more gently, with time to think (over half-term, for example) would have been kinder. Do I have feelings for this strange girl who talks to no-one? She is pretty, in a sort of wild animal kind of way. But I am very nearly twice her age as well as her teacher. I shudder at the enormity of it. But Tracey can't be lying; she is on a mission, and is far too convinced of what she is saying for that.

The fact that her arch-rivals have entered the equation gives me even more cause for worry. Actually, I no longer know what is disturbing me the most. I only know that my hollow stomach groans in protest as the knots gnarl. It is not a feeling I like.

94

The Mountain

Speaking with Judy Hartington is not a prospect I like, either. At the very best of times I would be unlikely to describe it as my favourite activity, and this is very definitely not the best of times. But I feel a sort of pre-emptive strike on my part might be in order. The rumour-factory, I have learned, works quickly in a school; in a few days, this rumour will be widespread. I would be wise to get my denial in first, or rather second – Tracey's enemies were no doubt first with their take on events half-way through lesson one this morning. It is important that I go around quashing this story before it gathers a momentum of its own.

During afternoon break I walk across the schoolyard to the cold metallic building of B block, where the English department is housed. As I climb the steps to her room at the top, B24, I look around me for any excuse not to continue. A boy not wearing a tie is challenged where this would normally go unchecked, in the interest of pure procrastination rather than any interest in his sartorial elegance. I have knocked on the doors of dentists' surgeries with more enthusiasm than I do at room B24, and I pray to myself that she is not in.

"Yes?"

I enter.

"*Nigel!* Well, hello, stranger. What brings you to the distant murky shores of B block?"

"Well, it's business...sort of."

"Intriguing. Come into the rim. Tea?"

"Um, OK."

"Darjeeling? Lapsang-souchong?"

"*What?*"

Her laugh tinkles like a bell. If the door were open, I'm sure it would peal all the way down the stairway.

95

The Mountain

"Oh, you are funny, with your naïve little unwordly-wise ways. They're only kinds of tea, not Eastern sexual practices."

Something about the thought makes me shudder. In my confusion I lapse into the vernacular of the children.

"*Whatever.*"

She lets out a laugh again. The kids nearby will think the next lesson has started.

"Oh, I *do* like the way you say that. It's…*sweet.*"

I think, but don't say, 'if I had wanted to be patronised I would have stayed in my own departmental area; Anthony does the job very nicely. There's always Gillespie, if he gets tired.' Instead I smile wanly.

"I'm in a bit of a pickle."

Judy sits up and looks grave, to show me that I have her full, undivided attention.

"Go on, Nigel. You can tell *me.*"

"Well, it's a bit embarrassing." I pause. "It's very embarrassing."

"Go on."

"Those girls this morning on cover, in Art." I don't know how to say this; it doesn't sound right.

"Which girls?"

"The ones sitting talking to you. All the second half. One looks like a pig."

"Yes?" She shoots me a quizzical, 'I'm-very-busy-but-I'm-quite-intrigued' kind of look. "Go on."

"Well, the thing is…they're trying to get someone in trouble."

"Oh really?"

"Yes. Anna Lomas, the self-elected mute. There's a feud."

"How can you have a feud with someone who doesn't talk?"

"They can, trust me. I mean, they are."

"And I need to know this because…?"

The Mountain

"They're saying they caught her and me...kissing." My head is hot and red. "They say she and I are…having an affair." This isn't actually quite true, as far as I know, but by disarming it before it is even suggested then I am having my say first, and hopefully nipping it before it gets to the bud.

"Why *Nigel!"* she exclaims, and at first I think she is happy for me. Then her face turns grim. "What utter, *utter* nonsense."

The sweat pours down my face as I nearly cry with relief.

"Well, I know, but…"

"Now, there, Nigel," she coos, as if comforting a small child crying, but the liquid emanating from my face is pure sweat, nothing else.

"It's just that…well, I wondered whether you might have thought-"

"Don't be silly, Nigel. A good-looking boy like you, and that moody little tart." She moves unnervingly closer to me. "*Very* good-looking, and available. You kid do better for yourself…"

After what I hope is a respectable interval of time, I thank her, leave the classroom and bolt down the stairway at full speed. The sweat is positively pouring off me, but the relief is incredible. Every bone in my body aches with the tension of the last few hours. Pupils stare at me as I run down the stairs three at a time.

My next lesson flies by, I barely notice the time, I am a mere spectator. All day long I've had the unsettling feeling that I am watching myself from elsewhere and not really present at all. But now the lesson flies by because I am in the throes of euphoric relief. At the end of the day I am ready to forget about the events of the last few hours, and those of a week ago, when I spot a small girl coming towards me, pushing her way through the tide of pupils rushing in the opposite direction. She bears a note, which she hands to me. On it is written:

97

The Mountain
'Why you ignoring me? Don't you care?

My life has been turned upside down. I might have to leave home. And school. Don't you even care?

Can you meet me at 6 tonight at the entrance to the Park?

From A.'

Chapter 10

Becky's worried. I can tell when Becky's worried. We're mates. We're walking to school, having an early morning fag, and she goes, "What was you thinkin' of? People saw you!" I do sometimes talk to Becky, but not now. Can't think of what to say. I'm worried. 'Course I'm worried. Been worried since that Friday. But Becky won't tell me what to do. So she's cluckin' away at me, peckin' me head, givin' it this an' that, I goes, "Leave it, eh, Becky!" That usually works, that's like *more* than enough, but not now. Not this morning.

"What was you *thinkin'*?" she drones on, an' I'm getting tired of this record. "A teacher! Not even a lad from school, or off The Park – a *teacher.* That's sick. That's gross. I never liked him. He's a slime ball."

But we've been through this before. He's not a slime ball; he's showed me the only bit of tenderness and care anyone has since God knows when. And it's not right that Becky didn't like him – she did. So did Tracey; so does Tracey. Of course what happened was stupid, or at least, how an' where it happened were. We were smashed and picked a 'phone booth on the main road into town, of all places. It was stupid, but that don't make it *wrong.* And even if it did, it's happened now, so that's tough.

I had a shit half-term – the worst ever. Everything after that night went wrong. Of course I never found out who trashed our caravan that Friday night – Dad was like a

99

complete stranger the next day, more distant than ever, we just went about the job of cleaning up the mess in silence. Poor Darren was in bed for two days, just sat there whimpering, I've never seen him so bad. Of course, he's petrified, but of what, I'll never know – he won't say. Didn't see his mates all weekend, didn't go out nicking or nowt, just lay there in bed with his bruises. Sometimes I lay there in bed with him, we just lay there and cuddled.

Of course Charon never got in touch – how could he? He's not exactly gonna come on to the Park lookin' for me. Even if he did, he doesn't have a clue how to find me, and there's no 'phone. I can't blame him, he even asked on that night if we could meet again, but we both knew we couldn't. Who knows, maybe we never will. I still feel let down, like he's deserted me, although I know that's not right, 'cos he couldn't find me. But did he even try to? I doubt it. I feel let down.

I could have done with someone to talk about what happened in the caravan that night, that is someone apart from Tracey and Becky. Anyway, they seemed more interested in the gossip about me and Charon. No point denying anything to them. By the sounds of things, no point denying anything to anyone no more, but someone better start pretty sharpish, and I don't talk.

For about twenty minutes that Friday night, I felt more alive and more real than I have at any time since Eddie's death. That's not much out of a life, is it, twenty minutes? But it's meant more to me than anything for a very long time. And yet since that night, I don't think I've ever felt so bad about things since Eddie died, too. My family's nothing – I can't cope with living with Dad, I'm obviously no good at looking out for Darren, and Mum's long gone. I can forget school. No-one gives me a chance, I've hardly any mates, and now I've been seen by half the town goin' with my form teacher. That'll look great on a reference. To top it all I don't even know if he cares, so it's maybe best I never see him again. It's best I leave.

The Mountain

Normally Becky's chuntering and peckin' me head would have done my head in completely by now, but I haven't really been listening. It's all gone over me head, me mind's on other things. So we reach the school gates without me having killed her, and light up one more fag before goin' in. Some of the hard lads on the leisure centre steps are callin' my name and giving us funny looks.

That's nothin' compared to registration. It all goes dead silent when we go in the room. People whispering and sniggering, but the silence, which is never usually there, tells me there's something well wrong. And Charon doesn't even look at me. Something's really wrong – why wouldn't he look at me? Not a word, not a look, nowt. That hurts me. I'm growin' sensitive in my old age. And he has a chance. Becky's gone now and stopped mitherin' me, but Tracey and I stay behind for a minute after registration, as we sometimes do. Not a word.

Some god or something is playing tricks on me. We have Art first, and who's on cover, only Charon. I hate Art, 'cos I'm in a class with those evil bitches from hell Emma Beswick and Karen Hurst and their mates, and it's the kind of lesson where you can talk a bit anyhow, and they're always havin' a go at me and Tracey. I know, even though I was wasted, I know they were around that night. They'll have seen us. Might as well put an ad in the local paper.

Charon has no control anyhow, and so chat is what they do. You'd need to be deaf not to hear some of what they're saying. Tracey is up at his desk bendin' his ear, and I can guess what that's about, an' all. And those two evil bitches keep giving me dead eyes, like they could normally care about me an' what I get up to. They just want to stir and wreck my life.

At the half-bell there's worse – way worse. That cow Hartington comes in. She's assistant head of year 5,

101

and thinks she has all the girls' confidence – 'you know, girls, you can tell me *anything.'* Except she can be a mardy cow whose mood changes are unpredictable, and I don't trust her. She's a gossip and a stirrer. Takes one to know one and before two minutes have gone she's been approached by Bitch Beswick and Whore Hurst, and they're there at her desk like three witches, plotting an' scheming. This time they're a bit craftier, I can only hear bits, but I know from the dead eyes they're talking about me, and I know from the way they are what they'll be telling the one who says you can tell me anything. This worries me loads – it won't stop here. She'll make it her business to tell half the school by this morning break.

I feel miserable and I feel sick. Does Charon even care? Everyone else has something to say about that night, but not him. He's in deep trouble, they might sack him. I don't even think he knows, or if he does, I don't know if he cares. As for me, I might as well never see him again.

That morning break I find out something else I'm going to have to live with – my troubles are only just beginning. I go to the loo and there's Hurst and her bitch mates.

"Ooh, look who it is," goes one.

"Ooh, if it ain't little miss teacher-shagger!"

"What were he like, Lomas? Were he any good?"

"What's the matter, teacher's pet? Lost your tongue?"

"She hadn't lost her tongue that night! It were wrapped round his tonsils, we seen it!"

"Who didn't?"

They push me around a bit. I hate this. They're clever enough not to do it too hard at first, just a bit of banter, bit of pushin' and shovin'. That way if a teacher comes in, or if someone grasses to a teacher, it's like 'Oh, it's only a bit of fun and games. High spirits. Handbags at six paces. Rough and tumble. Six of one and half a dozen of the other.' Well I'm sick of it. It's like, ten of them and none of me, that's what it is. They push me an' shove me and pinch me where the teachers can't see, kick me when we're alone 'cos they say I'm weird. Then a teacher comes and it's all 'Oh, miss, we're only havin' a laugh. We're mates. She's our mate.' The hell I am, I don't have mates, not in that way. And they kick me some more, maybe nick one of my bracelets, yank out an earring as rough as they can.

I try and push them away.

"What's the matter, Lomas? Going to run and tell your form tutor?"

One of them then takes on a serious tone. It's Beswick.

"Now you listen to us, bitch. We seen you. We all seen you, right? You and that teacher twat. We've spoken to Hartington and she believes us. She believes *us*. Know what that makes you an' lover boy? Finished. Dead meat. History, like your skanky brother's history."

At this I fly at the evil bitch and reach for her eyes with my long filthy nails. I'm this far away; if there wasn't three of them holding me back, I'd have ripped her eyes out. It'll take more than three to hold me for long, though. I struggle to get near enough to the bitch, take a run at her and the weight of me and the three who're trying to hold me pin her against the wall in a corner. I step hard on one toe, knee her crotch, and then bite her in the face as hard as I can. Her friends have to pull me away from her cheek. The skin is bright red, the teeth marks white and deeply indented, and blotches of blood appear on the surface.

Her friends hold me back but I break loose. Then Beswick flies at my hair, she's pullin' and tuggin' at it, yankin' out great long strands of it, pullin' it so hard my eyes are crying and I feel that my head's gonna split open. She's pullin' and pullin' and she drags me down on to the floor by pullin' at my hair. Now I'm on the floor and it

103

stinks and she's rubbin' my face into the grime on the
floor, you can tell it's real serious now 'cos her mates have
gone all silent, no cheering or braying for blood now. It's
silent. She's got massive chunks of my hair in her hands as
she rubs my nose into the floor. Then she stops for a
breather and I swipe her face with the back of my hand and
must have caught her cheek with one of my chains, 'cos
she cries out and there's a massive scar across her one of
her cheeks to go with the bite mark on the other one. I'm
encouraged by how bad she looks and I get to my feet now
and reach for one of her ears. I grab it in my hand and
twist it, then place my index finger and thumb around her
earring and pull as hard as I can. I can *hear* the tissues in
her skin beginning to rip, then she lets out the most
bloodcurdling scream I ever heard. I am stopped before I
can rip the ring right through her ear, I am pulled off once
again, but her ear-lobe has stretched to about six inches, it
feels like it has stretched all the way down to the *floor,* and
she's lyin' there all broken, beaten and bloody, and I know
she won't be troublin' me for a while.

   The door flies open and I hear a voice: "Right,
everyone out!" and I recognise through my matted, tear-
swollen eyelids one of the people I least want to see in the
whole world, bitch Hartington.

   "You two girls, pick yourselves up, now. To Dr
White's office!"

   I feel a wreck. I console myself that Beswick
might look worse. My head is stinging. I bet her ear is.
'Dr White's office' is meant to like really scare us, it's the
ultimate threat here. I'm not the least bit bothered. I'll get
suspended, that's OK, he's less scary than Gillespie by far.
When he says something, I don't for a second get the
feeling he means it.

   So Hartington makes us wait just outside and goes
in to talk to him. I could do without this bit. She hates me,

she's been talking to Beswick and her grubby mates about me half the morning, and what if she lets on to old man White. After what seems like half an hour the great man finds time to see us. He hauls Beswick in first, which I don't like. Five minutes later he calls for me.

"And what, young lady, do you have to say for yourself?"

He should know better; he really should.

"You must understand that we simply cannot tolerate fighting in this establishment. If you and your peers want to remain a member of this school then you must abide by the rules. If you cannot be relied upon to abide by the rules you must be excluded. I therefore have no option but to suspend you for five days. A letter will be sent home to your father with whom you must attend a re-admission interview after the five-day period before you can be re-admitted."

He's making a lot of assumptions here: I don't want to remain a member of his skanky school and couldn't give a toss for his precious rules. I care even less about what he can or cannot tolerate in his establishment. And Dad comin' up to school – like *that's* gonna happen. It never has yet, so as for it happening now… But this guy likes to hear himself talk, so I let him. I feel faint, and his office is warm, but I can sit down, so I might as well let him talk.

"*Most* unladylike behaviour."

After two minutes I'm out of there. I have some forms I'm supposed to take to Gillespie's office and the main office, well stuff that. I'm suspended as it is, how much *more* suspended can I be? I'm supposed to remain in isolation within the premises until the end of school today, but I'll be that much *more* isolated if I'm off the premises, so I'm doin' them a kind of favour. I go and get my bag and am out of the gates within five minutes of leaving the creep's office, heading for a fag outside the leisure centre.

The Mountain

The leisure centre's a right dump. Dodgy-looking blokes with no jobs hang around and play pool. But for me, it's safer than goin' home, Dad might be in during the day. I'll hang around here for a while, have a coffee and a smoke to steady my nerves, maybe go on a run.

I wait there 'till 12. I have an arrangement with Becky and Tracey that if ever I go missing I'll meet them either at the leisure centre or in the precinct. They're not meant to go out of school at dinner but it's right across the road and everyone does. And right enough, at 12, they both come into the snooker room. It's safe there; it's out of bounds to the school which don't mean owt, but there's less chance of being seen than on the steps.

Tracey's like, "What happened to *you?* What're you like?? Look at you!" Becky's like, "You should see that cow Beswick! She's in a right state. She's half dead!" It's suddenly real nice to see them, like it isn't only an hour since I last saw them, and like they haven't spent half of today doin' my head in, tellin' me what's best for me. They're my only mates, and it's nice to see them. But I don't want to talk so much, so I goes, "Pass this note on to Charon. Don't one of you do it, though, that's well risky. Get someone else to see he gets it."

Tracey's like, "You need to get home and get some rest!" I'm like, "yeah, *right!* I'll have the maid make up the bed and book me into my private clinic after afternoon tea." But they're my mates and I'm glad they came. As they leave I goes, "See you in the precinct! Either today or tomorrow."

I'm on a run. I'm on a long run. I changed into some running gear at the leisure centre, that's another good thing about it. I'm on a long run up to Mam Tor, the shivering mountain, the mother rock. It'll take me most of the afternoon.

The Mountain

I'm running up the steep mud path to the top of Brown Hill, with the Cross on my left. Clouds are gathering and it's already getting darkish. I'm knackered before I start, but feel better with each step. I especially love being out here when I know I should be in school.

So out along the ridge of Brown Hill, up past the TV mast, past a couple of farms, then I stop to look back at the town below – sad, grey slate rooftops in the drizzle. I feel good now. I run a bit more, past some wasteland, then down a drop onto tarmac and along near the railway line for a while. Then up the long, twisting path up Rushup Edge, up to Mam Nick, then a spectacular view of the valleys opening out on both sides. There's no-one else here, no-one for miles around, Mam Nick is the top of the world. Then along the long ridge up to Mam Tor. Near the top I rest a bit, and look down at the broken road on my right. A huge landslide swept away the whole road a few years ago, all the way down into the village, and if you run down it there are craters all over the place like on the surface of the moon. The craters are so deep and so long that you have to go around or take a massive jump. If you land in one you really struggle to get out.

Last time I was up here, last year, I was also bunkin' off school, although without being suspended into the bargain. I followed the broken road all the way down into the village, without stopping once. Near the village, where the holes aren't quite as big, I played a game for the last fifty yards. I took one long look at the ground, tried to memorise it, then ran those last fifty yards with my eyes closed, as fast as I could. I was terrified of landing in a hole, but excited by the risk. A sort of running roulette. Without knowing how I landed in one piece on the proper road that leads into the village.

Today though I keep running up the ridge, I can see for miles either side of me even though the weather's not good. Villages, factory chimneys, quarries sprawl out before me. I'm well above the trees now, perhaps a couple

107

The Mountain

of crazy Rowan trees but that's it, with only the wind for company. The wind pulls at me, jostles me, eggs me on in a friendly kind of way, and is my companion up along the Great Ridge. And the wind doesn't care when I don't talk back.

I'm at the top; two hours on my watch since I left town. So I've achieved something today, after all. You can still see the remains of an Iron Age Fort up here, the ramparts. They had funerals up here, too. I remember sitting in a warm classroom, in our Juniors, next to the radiator. I remember last thing on a wet, windy Friday afternoon when I was nine, Miss Phillips reading us a story about Mam Tor, the shivering mountain. I'm surprised at how much I remember, I can remember every single detail – not just of the story, but of the classroom, of the radiator, of the table I sat at, and of the lines on Miss Phillips' kind old face.

I don't know why, but this memory makes me so sad. It's a nice memory, but I want to cry. And I do, it makes me cry. I think back to the time when I loved school, when I was a bright little girl who the teachers liked. Miss Phillips called me her little friend, she looked out for me, and I paid her back; I remembered every word of every story she told me, every word of every song she sang. And I remember running home happily at the end of the day, full of stories to tell my mum. I remember a time when we were happy, when we had a family. I remember warm radiators and friends when I talked.

An' I look round, and it's already dark, and the lights are coming on in the distant villages, people are putting on the lights in their homes and sitting by the radiator. An' I turn to face the cold, howling wind, an' the tears are flowing right down my cheeks.

Chapter 11

The main Park is not to be confused with Coombs Moss Park, although they are both referred to as simply 'The Park'. I know that Anna lives on Coombs Moss Park, which is also known as Tintown – a grubby little caravan park on the edge of town with its own permanent population of a dozen or so families. The other park is Pavilion Park. Both parks are flattered somewhat by their grandiose names, but I know which park Anna has in mind. The main park is down near the centre of town and I make my way in that direction at six o'clock.

The rain has turned to hail and a bleak fog shrouds the trees and lawns of The Park. A cold black figure is already standing huddled in the gloom. I am suddenly extremely nervous and the thought strikes me that, with the exception of the night of the concert, we have never even spoken. A lot has happened.

"Anna?" I venture. The fog is so thick I could be mistaken, and part of me hopes that I am. There is no reply.

"Is that you, Anna?" Through the fog I can just about discern her shape and features, then something makes me start. Her face seems somehow misshapen. Her eyes are bruised, her mouth swollen, and there is something wrong with her hair as well. She looks even more ghostly and undernourished than usual, and I feel uneasy.

"What happened?" I ask helplessly. I want to take her in my arms. There is dried blood around her mouth.

The Mountain

She shrugs and breathes out quickly through her nose. This is as much of an answer as I am going to get. I seize my courage.

"Why did you want to meet me?" I may as well be asking the fog. "This is difficult for me. I *do* care. Please don't think that I don't care, I care a lot. It's just…well, I've never been in a position like this before. This is unchartered territory for me."

Why did I tell her that? My words are empty, they have no point. 'Care' is such an empty and useless verb. Anna's stubborn silence is a thousand times more eloquent than all my empty words put together.

I was sitting in the barn doing what I did best: nothing. My thesis was making no progress. I spent the days wandering aimlessly in the cool mountain air or else sitting there in the barn, staring into empty space. The evenings I would divide between drinking rancid red wine at the Bar-Jean or staring absent-mindedly at Marcia.

I decided I didn't really want to be with Marcia but lacked the courage to tell her; I could tell her in my head but the words simply wouldn't come out. They were paralysed somewhere in my throat; not even in my throat, they didn't even get that far, they were paralysed in my head.

I felt guilty about what happened to Marcia, she suffered because of her involvement with me. I also feared the revenge of her family if I were to abandon her. It was not quite the same fear as Paolo bearing down on me in the early hours of the morning with his clothing covered in another man's blood, but it was still fear. Quite simply, you were either on the side of Marcia's brothers or you were against them. For as long as I was with Marcia, she and I were the wronged victims. If I were to leave her I would get the punishment that was waiting for Paolo. I felt sick as I thought of it. Paolo was going to take my

110

punishment, he would be sacrificed so that I might be spared.

The guilt was terrible, and I think that accounted for the paralysis of my words. I had stood before Marcia, meaning to tell her – I had told her so often in my dreams – and the words failed me. I was impotent. In fact, the words were all there. I had failed the words.

In a contrary act, I picked up one of my German books I had with me and turned the pages idly and apathetically, and my eyes fell on the crude, naïve underlinings of an eager undergrduate at what must have been a key passage. The words jumped up at me from the yellow page: 'Worte, Worte, Worte – sie erreichen mich nicht.' That was it!

The main character, Paul, was home on leave from the western front. He was looking through his old and familiar school books and felt alienated and excluded from everything. Nothing moved him, nothing reached him. The words were there but they could not communicate. The words could not reach him.

I don't know how long we have been here. I look helplessly at Anna. She has still not spoken. My words are out there somewhere, being carried off into the cold evening air, being battered by the hail or enveloped by the fog, or both, but they haven't reached Anna.

"Anna," I try again, for about the fifth time. "Say something. Have I let you down? Are you angry with me?"

The fog has lifted a little and I can see her dark eyes. She has been crying. Her cheek is badly swollen and discoloured. And she nods her head slowly. And she turns and disappears into the fog.

The Mountain

"We must have...*supper* together one of these days, you and I," says Dr White the next day in a sinister tone. "I do a very nice...Spaghetti *Bolognese.* Yes, Spaghetti *Bolognese,* I think," he muses to himself as he walks on down the corridor.

I baulk at the thought of an evening 'tête à tête' with the one they call Dr Death. His idea of a convivial 'soirée' and mine may not, I fear, match, and the manner of his no doubt well-meant invitation, with its dramatic pauses and strange emphasis on certain key words does not make me any keener on the idea.

I can't really concentrate on socialising as it is. I feel wretched about Anna, haunted with guilt about my inaction and what she must see as lack of concern. She has been beaten up and excluded from school, and the one person, or one of the few persons, with whom she has spoken in the last year has let her down. And she can no longer speak to him, and he can't speak to her. He tries to, but his words don't reach.

The more my words don't work, the more critical I am of the way in which other people use their own. It is as if everyone has so many words and no more, and they are aimlessly and thoughtlessly squandering their allocation. Anthony is master of the cliché, and I am beginning to become impatient with him. I am becoming a pedant. For example, after school on Wednesday there was a staff versus pupils football match. I scored twice in an improbable 7-5 victory. Anthony approaches me the next morning at school, full of his usual bonhomie:

"Nice *goals!*"

"Pardon?"

"Your brace last night – magic! Talk of the staffroom!"

"Did you see them?"

"Pardon?"

112

The Mountain

"I asked whether you saw them."

"Well, I…"

"Did you see the goals?"

"Well, no, not really."

"Not *really*? So in what way did you see them?"

"Well, I didn't *actually* see them."

"So how do you know whether they were nice or not?"

"Well…"

This conversation trails off, and afterwards I feel really petty. Anthony has tried to be friendly and I have taken exception to his empty words. On another occasion he is comparing the coursework of two pupils:

"Gill Kingsley and Sam Hitchens. You wouldn't think they were from the same planet!"

"Pardon?"

"Gill Kingsley and Sam Hitchens. They both have had ten days to come up with 150 words about their home area in French. Look at this and look at that. There's just no comparison."

"There is."

"Pardon?"

"There is. You've just made it."

"Pardon?"

"You said look at this and look at that. That's a comparison. One's in blue ink and the other's in black. That's another comparison. So you can't say 'there's no comparison'. You *can* say it, but you shouldn't."

I find myself very tiresome at moments like this. Anthony is well-meaning and his slapdash approach to language makes him a very soft target. I am being pompous and arrogant; I am turning into David Stanton. The other staff, I can feel, don't really like it and I don't really blame them. How can someone so unassertive and hesitant inside the classroom be so dogmatic with a senior member of staff, with a harmless old well-loved institution like Anthony?

113

The Mountain

My mood towards Gillespie is no better, although it is more justified. He reports scathingly about Anna's exclusion during morning briefing and is incapable of resisting the temptation to put his opinions into the equation:

"Ladies and gentlemen, by now you will have heard that Anna Lomas and Emma Beswick have been excluded for five days for fighting. A most unladylike display it was too and the kind of behaviour which, ladies and gentlemen, we will not tolerate at Chapelton High School. The Lomas girl has been in trouble on numerous occasions and she is a bad influence on others. It would be better all round if this sort of trailer trash were to look for a school elsewhere, quite frankly."

After briefing I approach Gillespie. I am nervous but I take him on.

"Why trailer trash?"

"Pardon?"

"Why did you call Anna Lomas trailer trash?"

He looks unsettled and hesitates before answering.

"She's nothing but trouble. One of these traveller families. Live up on that godforsaken Coombs Park. Father's an alcoholic. Wouldn't *you* describe that as trailer trash?"

I am surprised at how calm I am and I, too, hesitate.

"No, it so happens that I wouldn't. I'm her form tutor and may know more about her than you do. She holds that family together, by all accounts, cooking and cleaning for them."

"She could start by cleaning herself."

"She has nothing going for her. She has to do all the housekeeping. They were almost penniless throughout the miners' strike, brother died, and mum left."

We are attracting a little audience by now but I have unwittingly shot myself in the foot by mentioning the miners' strike.

114

The Mountain

"The miners' strike!" Gillespie echoes sarcastically. "What would *you* know about *that*? If you'd been here, instead of poncing around at university, you might be in a position to comment. An industry which was dying on its feet, and which would have died a long while ago were it not for government hand-outs, tried to hold the country to ransom and was joined by rent-a-mob yobs in a disorganised attempt to undermine the forces of law and order. They deserve everything they got."

"That family has been torn apart. No-one deserves to live in Coombs Park, no-one deserves a dead brother and an absent mum. The girl is the sole carer for the family. Without her they wouldn't even eat. Perhaps this school should show a little compassion."

I sound horribly sanctimonious and compound the impression by walking out of the staffroom. Perhaps some will agree with me, perhaps I have made myself another enemy. Anthony and Gillespie have in common that they are both to some extent victims of my inability to communicate with Anna.

"Ut si," proclaims David Stanton that evening in the Swan. "You were having a bit of a go at old Gillespie, weren't you? Which must make it your round."

Impressed by this logic I go to the bar. When I return Lou and Geoff are also at the usual table.

"Fancy an argument?" Geoff asks me. "I never had you down as a Scargill supporter. He wouldn't have a ballot, you know."

I am weary.

"He was elected," I begin, going through the motions. "Leaders who are elected don't have a ballot every time a decision has to be made, they were elected to make the decisions."

"He should have listened to the membership."

The Mountain

"He was representing their views. If they didn't like it, tough. They should have protested." I am getting a little bored by now and want to change tack. "Were there many demonstrations in this area in the mid-eighties?"

"We haven't been here much longer than you," replies Geoff. "But there was some solidarity amongst the staff for Scargill. And the community, well most of them were behind him."

Eleanor Whiting and Judy Hartington enter the pub.

"What about them?" I ask, more for something to say than out of any interest.

Everyone around the table roars with laughter.

"Them!" exclaims David. "I *think* you'll find that they're not particularly *engagées* as far as that kind of thing goes. Don't be fooled by the feminist earrings. The only thing they'd protest about would be if Marks and Spencers ran out of taramasalata."

I am not particularly fond of this image but it diverts attention from me and my fracas in the staffroom.

"Anyway as a subversive revolutionary you'll be looking forward to Sunday," says Lou. This passes as an averagely obscure remark for him so draws no comment from anyone, until he prods me so persistently that I realise he has been talking to me.

"Guy Fawkes Day," he adds conspiratorially.

As a result of our conversations I am persuaded to have a small party in my flat on Sunday evening. The back yard is just about big enough for a bonfire and Geoff and Lou bring some fireworks. The air is rancid and yellow with the combined smell of burning sulphur and the sausages I have attempted to cook. It is no surprise that on their entry, Judy and Eleanor appear even in this bad light to have their noses haughtily held towards the air.

116

The Mountain

"Joining the bachelor boys," says Judy, but there is something curious about her delivery. Eleanor laughs supportively. She has apparently selected a tablecloth to wear for this evening's entertainment. Their perfume is overpowering and appears unafraid of doing battle with the existing aromas. The girls stagger precariously on inappropriate footwear and head for my kitchen. Raucous laughter emerges.

"Someone seems happy," is Geoff's analysis.

"And why wuild I not be?" replies Judy on her return in an unconvincing Caledonian accent. Minutes later the inevitable rain drives us inside as well. The bonfire is left to smoulder, the few remaining fireworks are sitting in a soggy box.

Judy has a half-empty bottle of white wine in one hand and a full glass of red wine in the other. Eleanor is rolling a cigarette, which I have never before seen her do and which she may well be doing for the first time, judging by her efforts. As she turns around to acknowledge us Judy knocks a plate with potato salad onto the floor, and I notice why their entry had seemed odd at first. Both Judy and Eleanor are completely, unmistakeably drunk.

"Sorry, Nigel," giggles Judy. "I'll clean up for you later?"

"I bet you will!" cackles Eleanor, and the ensuing hilarity makes me think I have missed either some sophisticated *double-entendre* or failed to spot some coded in-joke.

"Christ, what have you two been drinking?" It is Geoff who articulates the question on everyone else's mind.

"Oh, this and that," Eleanor replies mysteriously. She is not usually the spokesperson for the pair but this evening seems the more sober, and is consequently put in charge of the words. "We had Sunday lunch at colleagues of Frances – Judy asked me at the last minute as one of the wives had to cancel. A dreadful affair, but flowing in

117

The Mountain

booze. Cocktails in the conservatory, that kind of thing. After lunch some of them went to the Castle Hotel for pre-theatre drinks – very splendid too. The two events just rolled into one. And now, consequently - here we are."

We are all struck by the logic of this conclusion, and unusually, I am the first to react.

"Who's Frances?"

"Judy's man." A sardonic grunt can be heard.

"Where's Frances?"

This time the grunt precedes the words, although they may not be imparted by the same person.

"He had a Mason's meeting, would you believe. On a Sunday afternoon! He met a few of them at the golf club, God knows where they are now."

"Who cares?" This time it is Judy.

"So, we just drank and drank. Judy gets fed up when he has these meetings anyway, but on Sunday…"

Judy steadies herself against the table, raises the glass in her right hand, and slurs:

"Cheers! Here's to Guy bloody Fawkes!"

Eleanor asks me for a light for her cigarette, which she seems to have remembered. As she follows me into the living room where the ashtrays are kept, she tugs at my arm.

"We do like you, you know."

"Pardon?"

"Oh, you and your pardons! We like you!"

"There's a relief."

"Oh, I know we tease you and laugh at you, for your naïve little ways and your pardons and your uselessness in the classroom, but, well, we like you, that's what."

"Good." I am a bit miffed, firstly at having been teased, but more so at not having noticed.

She lurches forward and leans against me.

"Especially Judy."

118

The Mountain

This sounds ominous and I feel I had better change the topic of conversation.

"You'll find lighters and ashtrays in here," I inform her.

At about 11 the party shows signs of drawing to an end. Eleanor has reached the stage where she can drink no more, a stage Judy reached several hours before.

"Are you going anywhere near Duke's Close?" she asks Geoff.

"Vaguely. Want to walk with me?"

"Please. That might be gid. I might not find it by myself."

"What about your friend?"

"Normally, I'd say she can speak for herself? Tonight, I'm not so sure. She lives miles away."

"I know, that's why I asked."

Eleanor turns to me.

"She lives about 10 miles away, right up a mountain, halfway up Black Ridge. I don't know how she'll get back? Her husband's out with his Mason cronies, and even if he wasn't, they were hardly speaking earlier on. They always argue when he's out with his Masons, and she always drinks like a fish when they argue." Given her own state of sobriety, Eleanor has summed the situation up surprisingly logically. Then she sidles up to me and whispers: "Can she stay here?" She squeezes my arm before I can answer and turns to Judy and shrieks: "Nigel says you can stay here. But behave yourself!"

The party breaks up at about 11.30. I arrange for Judy to sleep on the sofa-bed in the living room. She has sheets and a bowl in case she is sick. I go to the bathroom and on returning to my room see her, pale and serious-looking, standing in the doorway.

"Sleep with me," she says.

119

Chapter 12

The meeting in the Park with Charon is a complete waste of time. He's standing there and he's saying nothing. What is the point of all his caring if he can say nothing. He's really let me down. I don't know why, but I'm surprised.

The run up to Mam Tor was the only good thing in my day. After that it really was all down hill. I gets back about 4 and Dad's only in. Chances of that are about one in a million. So I tells him I've gone an' got myself excluded, fightin', and he goes ballistic. Like, he never fought or owt when he was younger. I goes to him that she was slaggin' off the family, him an' the family, but it's like he's deaf. He's shoutin' an' screamin' an' chuckin' stuff, sayin' you're not my daughter' an' 'what would your mum say' an' all this stuff. And I've had enough, I've been picked on and shouted at enough for one day, so I tell him, and he smacks me real hard across the face. I'm stingin'. I call him a bastard, which really riles him, and he just can't stop chuckin' stuff at me – pots, pans, books, lamps. More miss me than hit me, but while I'm duckin' out the way I trip and smack my head really hard against the electric fire. I'm in a right mess. I gets up and I goes, "Dad, I'm off. I can't live with you like this. I'm sorry, I really am, but she started it. They all pick on me there, now you pick on me here. I'm up at 6 cleaning this dump and cook for you and all that and I have school to cope with. I can't take any more. I'm gonna leave, I'll look for Mum."

The Mountain

Then I runs out. Of course he's screamin' at me to come back. Darren's hiding under the bed sheets, cowering like a scared rabbit. And I goes to meet Charon.

Wish I never had. I need someone to talk about this stuff to, but he's useless. Just talks about himself, about how much he cares. I feel that my bruises and scars need a bit more than a couple of words. I really thought he cared before. He showed tenderness. I even fantasised that we might run away together. I don't know what's wrong. Is he scared for his career? Am I too much trouble? I'm really down and I need some help right now.

That night I need to meet either Becky or Tracey, 'course they're not in. So I goes down to the late shop to try an' skank a bottle of something, I'm not doin' the sweet-talking part and anyway I've no money. It's hard this, most of the booze is behind the counter, but the dorks have left out a few big cider bottles and amazingly they also sell some glue in this place. I just reach out an' grab – I don't even care, I don't care about nothin' no more – so I reach out an' grab and of course they notice me immediately. I'll be on CCTV an' all, but I still don't give a stuff, and armed with my bottle and tube of glue I run like hell for the door. Two shop assistants are after me, and follow me out the door, but they'll never catch me and the pigs are too thick to find my little hiding place.

So for now, I'm made. I run like mad towards the Park where I meet that useless Charon, using all the little back passages and ginnels of course, and the fog does a good job of hiding me as I open the bottle. I empty about a third of it straight down my neck, doesn't even touch my mouth, one gulp. Now the glue. I've got an' old paper back and stick my head into it as far as I can, then sniff an' sniff. The familiar dizzy feeling kicks in almost immediately, and everything's spinnin'.

The Mountain

Charon is a waste of space. He just spouts empty words the whole time. That's one of the reasons I don't even answer him. He don't care. He just stands there, talkin' at me, my head's spinning and I don't need this. I turn round to go, his meaningless words make a pathetic attempt to reach me but I know they never will. I'm best off without him and I go back for my bottle and glue.

Next second I hears voices. Well, I think it's next second, but I'm completely soaking wet, I'm drenched through and it's completely dark. The clock is chiming 9 o' clock! The voices are the sound I don't like to hear, they sound, well, like the voices of authority. How have they traced me to here? I see a torch, I hear a dog sniffin'. I'm nicked!

And just when I'm thinkin', these pigs can't be as thick as they look, I hear a voice:

"So this is where the father says the girl sometimes used to come, Mr Osborne?"

I'm well freaked. Clive ("Hey, call me Clive") Osborne. Our useless social worker. What the hell is he doing here? Well they won't get me. They probably couldn't even find the Park by themselves. Dad doesn't have a clue where I go to hang out, it may as well be the Christian Mothers' Union Sewing Circle for all he knows. It's a lucky guess. Well they've been dragged here by luck, but they can still make a mess of catching me, if I know them. I ain't coming out. But I feel uneasy – not just because Clive ("Hey, call me anytime, day *or* night") Osborne is useless, but his presence (rather than him himself, he's too useless) usually means trouble. What's he want here?

My blood goes cold even more at the sound of a second voice and I swear my heart stops. It is young, frail, and punctuated my sobs. It goes:

"She comes here to meet her mates and have a fag and a drink."

122

The Mountain

It's Darren. My whole body shudders and shivers with goose-pimples. Why's he here? And then I'm angry. Why's he dobbed me in? And then I'm scared. Why's he here, not Dad? Where's Dad? What's so bad that needs a social worker again? And then I'm angry again. I could have got away with this easily, but for bad luck (or their good luck). Has Dad been hitting Darren again? Has he taken his rage at me out on him? And I'm angry, scared, sad and guilty all at the same time.

I take the time to hide the cider bottle and glue bag under what feels like a bush, and step out of the trees I'd been hiding amongst. It feels like three or four torches are flashed at me, and then I see the blue sirens of their stupid pig cars. A dog is sniffin' at me, barking like the thick pig-mutt it is, and this voice says:

"Anna Lomas?"

Then I hear Darren, poor little Darren, caught up in this mess and it's not his fault, and I want to cry, and he goes:

"She don't talk."

In the pig-shop there's three pigs, a pig-woman, useless Clive Osborne, Darren and me. The pig-woman talks first:

"Anna, we have some bad news. Your father has disappeared. Darren alerted Mr Osborne at about 5 this evening. Apparently your father just packed his bags and left without saying a word. The police have, as you can see, been alerted and a search has begun. Of course, at this early stage there is absolutely no need for alarm, we will do everything we can to trace your father. In the meanwhile you will both go into temporary accommodation arranged by Mr Osborne. Your little brother showed considerable presence of mind this evening."

She's trying to be all understanding and as gentle as a Blue Peter presenter or something, but I just feel sick.

123

The Mountain

She's still waffling on about something or other, words
which have no meaning and don't reach me. And who
cares anyway? The bottom line is: I got myself excluded,
Dad slapped me, I got trashed, Dad got guilty and left, poor
Darren's caught up in the middle and now the family's a
bigger mess than ever. I hate Dad for abandoning us.
Mum already abandoned us, and we needed her way more
than we needed Dad. Right now, we need Dad 'cos he's all
we've got, and he's gone too. And did he hit Darren?
Probably. My thoughts are all mixed up. Poor Darren, too
loyal and too scared to dob in his own dad, probably only
dobbed in his sister's whereabouts 'cos he was even more
scared of being left alone. I feel I want to die.

"Of course, we'll keep you informed of any
developments," the pig-woman is saying.

So we traipse up to Combs Park with slime-ball
Osborne, the neighbours love this. We go into the caravan
and collect a few 'essential belongings' for the next few
days or weeks. It doesn't take us long, which is why I had
to laugh when the pig-woman said Darren had said Dad
had collected his belongings – how could he tell? What did
he have? Not much, to represent half a life.

Osborne's dumped us in some skanky hostel on
the other side of town, it's just as bad as the caravan but a
bit warmer, with proper walls. There again it's not home
and you can't just do what you want. You have to eat with
a group of other kids, you can't go out in the evenings, and
a fat woman shouts at you if you play music. You have to
go to school. Everyone here is in some kind of trouble, at
least you feel they are. Our little family in the caravan
didn't have much (it didn't have anything) but we were
together. Now everything's broken. Although I hate Dad,
I feel sad that he's left. I think Darren does too. But I
never see Darren in this place, which is big, and we sleep at
opposite ends of the building. I didn't think I'd mind that

124

as much as I do. He's in a room with some other kids, I hope they leave him alone. I'm by myself. Normally I'd like that, but at night I hear the girl in the next room crying herself to sleep, sniffling into her pillow, going, "Mummy" over and over again. It's eery and it gives me the creeps. I wish we were back in the caravan and I hate Dad again.

Every evening we have a smarmy oily family chat with Osborne. Except we're not family and I don't chat. The one good thing is it's about the only time I see Darren. They make us do therapy or something throughout the day and, because they agree that we've 'been through a lot, bless them', we're allowed to sleep quite a lot at first. Luckily they've agreed we don't have to go back to school for a few days, although there again 'cos I'm suspended it's not as great as all that. Anyway after all the therapies Osborne tries to be all cosy and asks us things like what we think the way forward for our family should be. The talks are a bit one-sided. He ends with a sentence like: "And if there's anything, *anything,* you'd like, just…" Just what? I don't tell him, but I have a list. Where should I start? My brother Ed back? My mum? Dad? For my face not to hurt? For Gillespie to die? For Charon to say what he means? To cuddle Darren at night, to look out for him?

We've been here since that first Monday after half-term. It's nearly Friday and there's no word of Dad. They're talking about me and Darren being ready for school on Monday of next week. I need to do something. Over the weekend I'll grab Darren and we'll discuss it. We don't have any therapies at the weekend and with any luck Osborne will keep his greasy nose out.

On Saturday morning we're all given a fiver and are walked into town into the precinct like we were mental or senile grannies or something. We have two hours. The first thing I want is not to buy fags, not to go nicking, not to 'phone my mates, but to spend five minutes alone with Darren.

"Oy, Daz! Here!"

"But we're going to Woolworths!"

"Chrissake! You can meet your mates in a minute. I need to talk to you." I never thought I'd say those last words to anyone, ever again.

"What?" He looks pained. I want to pick him up and cuddle him.

"Just…" Now the words begin to fail me. "How you doin'?"

"OK. Food's OK. Better than at home. I don't get picked on. Got a few mates. Got *this.*" He opens his sweaty hand to reveal his crumpled up £5 note.

"Is that all you care about?" I sound like somebody's mother. "What about Dad?"

He's silent.

"Dunno. And it's warmer." He hesitates again. "What about you?"

"I can't stay much longer. I need to find Dad. I know where he'll be."

"Yeah *right.*"

"Daz, I can find him. D'you wanna come?"

Darren looks at his fiver and looks at me. He *has* been through a lot.

"I'll stay here."

"OK listen. I don't get a chance to speak to you in that place, not alone. Listen."

Darren is looking round for his mates, and again at the fiver, like he's never seen one before.

"*Listen!* I'm going to sneak out and find Dad."

"How're you gonna do that?"

"I said, I know where he is."

"Liar. Anyway, I meant, how're you gonna sneak out?"

The Mountain

"On Sunday evening at tea-time they're having some sort of spazzy firework display in their crappy old back garden."

"It's a good garden. Better than-"

"Will you shut your face and listen!! Everyone will be there; while it's happening, I'll sneak out and look for Dad. Whatever happens, *I haven't told you anything.* Right?"

"So... why spend all this time telling me?"

"Christ!!" But I can't really think of an answer. Except, because I love you. I'll be thinking of you. I might not come back. I want you to know I'm thinking of you, that one day I'll be back to look out for you. That every night I go to bed I'll be thinking of your little head as it hits the pillow. But I can't say any of those things. Anyway, he's turned round and started to go and in his head he's already spending his fiver in Woolworths.

Sunday the shagging 5th November comes and so do the preparations for their spasticated firework display. We spend the afternoon collecting dry wood and cardboard for the fire, and some kids are busy stuffing a guy. Our minders are putting fireworks out in the garden in places where we can't reach them, ready to be lit when it gets dark. I am making my own preparations for when it gets dark. I've worked out that the front, side and back doors to this place are locked in the evenings – I spotted that on the first evening here. From the window of the upstairs loo, though, you can reach the metal fire escape ladder that goes down the side of the building. Most evenings the staff patrol all the corridors the whole time, so you can't even go to the loo without being followed, but tonight should be different. Tonight they think we're all watching their poxy fireworks.

At around 6 the entertainment begins. We are given a jacket potato and a glass of squash and most of

The Mountain

the kids are gathered round the fire to keep warm. It's beginning to rain and the wood on the fire is quite wet. I'm skulking in the background, which is what I do anyway. After about half an hour I sidle towards the door into the kitchen, which also leads to the staircase. Who's in the kitchen but bignose Osborne?

"Hello Anna! Are you enjoying yourself?"

He gets the answer he deserves, but that doesn't stop him trying again.

"Can we get you anything?"

I look around, alarmed, but he's using the patronising social-worker's we. I mime a drink of juice. He has to get it for me, of course.

"Anything else?"

I mime, as best I can, the actions of going to the loo. He's a bit slow but eventually cottons on.

"OK then! You know where to go by now! Don't be long, or you'll miss the Catherine Wheels and Jumping Jacks."

I'd love to speak, just to catch him out, just for once, so I could tell him where he can shove his Catherine Wheels and Jumping Jacks. But for now I'm racing up the stairs, three at a time, and making for the upstairs loo. At any time one of them could be patrolling.

Inside the cupboard in the loo, I've already hidden a small rucksack with some 'belongings'. I lift up the heavy sash window and squeeze out, legs first. It's lucky I'm skinny as a rat as it's a really tight squeeze.

Outside on the ledge my heart jumps into my mouth. The fire escape is way further than I thought. I'll have to swing right round or jump a bit, and we're four floors up. My arms and hands are trembling. But with my hands, I can reach up to grab onto the bottom of another ledge just above me, if I rest my feet on the window ledge. It's slippy and wet but I have to hurry.

The Mountain

I hear from inside someone knocking on the toilet door.

"Anna? You still in there, Anna? Everything alright?"

Everything's not alright so I jump and my hands clasp the wet slippy metal of the fire escape but then they slip a bit. I pull myself up onto it with all my strength and then half-run, half-slide down it. About thirty seconds later I'm at ground level and I can't believe I've made it without breaking any bones. Everything's not alright but I'm out of there, I'm out of here quicker than a social-worker can say 'rehabilitation', and I'm running off aimlessly into the night.

Chapter 13

"Nemo hic adest illius nominis," David is saying to someone outside the staffroom door. Suddenly he wheels around and sees me out of the corner of his eye and corrects himself. "I stand corrected, young lady. Mr Charon, a well-wisher at the door for you."

It's Becky, followed by an anxious looking Tracey.

"It's Anna," blurts Becky. "She's gone an' gone."

"I know. I heard about her exclusion."

"No." Becky looks more agitated. "I mean, *really* gone."

I must look puzzled. Tracey, as ever, is on hand to help.

"She's left the home she were in."

"What, that caravan?"

"No! *God!* You lot have your finger on the pulse!" This isn't like Tracey at all, so I sense that something really is wrong. "She only got taken into care. Her dad's left. She got taken into this hostel, run by social workers. She was meant to start back at school today. We were going to walk with her. Then, last night, police called round to mine and Becky's, saying, like, she's run off. Did we know where she might be, had she been in touch? Her little brother's going mental."

"That's what they *told* us," adds Becky, the voice of reason. "To make us feel bad, to make us tell. Only we can't tell, 'cos we don't know. We saw her in town, but she didn't say owt. As per usual."

"And then she left, last night, during their fireworks display," explains Tracey.

"Have you been in touch? Has she said anything to you at all?" asks Becky.

"No. I knew nothing of any of this."

Tracey stares at me. She looks really disappointed.

"Didn't you know, didn't you even know, that her dad had gone, and that she'd been taken into care?"

"No, I…how could I know?"

"Don't you even *care*?"

The last bit is unfair, and it stings, it stings like surgical spirit on an open wound. I retreat to the sanctuary of the staffroom.

I have been avoiding Judy Hartington all morning, so far with some success. This feat has not met with the same success where my other colleagues are concerned. Geoff is the first of last night's revellers to make a witty allusion to the welfare of my unexpected overnight guest.

"Well, old Judy's looking radiant this morning. You must have managed to be of some comfort to her in her state, *n'est-ce pas?*"

Eleanor reacts for her friend by proxy.

"She was in no state to go home. She's already told me what a…*gentleman* you were, Nigel. Thank you, thank you on her behalf."

Sniggers and guffaws meet this observation, and my case is not assisted by the fact that it is morning break in a crowded staffroom.

"I *think* that, " begins David, slowly and ponderously, "you just might find that Ms. Hartington seeks comfort from you on other occasions, so selfless were you in tending to her needs."

131

The Mountain

This is not what I want to hear, but Judy walking through the door the very next moment is not what I want to see, either. The staffroom goes quiet, more laughter is amateurishly suppressed and I suddenly wish I had some marking to be doing.

"Now then!" It is Anthony, and so my humiliation can be considered complete. His revenge for my recent offhand manner with him is timely. "Faint heart never won the hand of a fair lady, or something like that, eh, Nigel?" I want to return his amicable pat on the back with something a little stronger.

In spite of my best efforts, Judy catches me after lunch. I am free, as is she, and the staffroom is inconveniently empty.

"Nigel, are you avoiding me?" she begins, predictably.

"No, of course not."

"I hope I didn't impose on you too much last night."

"Impose? No, that's not the word I'd use."

She smiles. I'm trying to summon the courage to brush her off, to let her down gently, and she smiles.

"Did you enjoy our time together?"

"Yes."

"*Yes*? Can't you be any more forthcoming than that?"

"Yes, I enjoyed our time together."

She flickers her eyelids in a more pronounced way than is strictly necessary, and toys with her hair in what she must imagine to be a flirtatious, teasing manner.

"More of the same? Are we on for tonight?"

"Tonight's bad. Look, Judy, it was fun, I mean, it was great, but I don't really-

"Want to get too involved, I know." Judy is one of those people who feel they were put on this earth to

132

The Mountain

finish other people's sentences and it is particularly
irritating in this instance. "You young bucks just want to
have your fun. Well we girls do, too. I think we deserve a
bit of fun."

I feel weak, deprived of any argument I might
have had, and I feel confused. I do not fancy Judy, I do not
even like her. She is pushy and opinionated and normally I
would want to sleep with her as much as I would with
David. Last night's circumstances were not, I remind
myself, normal, but even so I am incapable of imagining
what possessed me to capitulate to her hungry and drunken
needs. There is not room inside my head for all of this, and
I want to escape.

I am preoccupied by what has happened to Anna,
in any event, and this is of considerably more concern to
me than the *affaire Hartington*, however irresistible she
thinks her *femme fatale*-like charms are. I am not as
unfeeling as Anna's friends think I am, not by any stretch
of the imagination, but I am unwilling to let them see how
affected I am. My carelessness has already nearly caused
considerable trouble and I cannot risk incriminating myself
further. At once I determine to arrest these thoughts – it is
Anna's welfare which must be of primary concern here.
Where is she? Is she safe? Is she sleeping rough? After
school I will go to her caravan and search the entire park.
Now, I want to hide inside a book, as my head already has
too many thoughts running around inside it. I am almost
pleased when the bell rings to announce the end of my free
lesson and to warn of the approaching lesson.

My 5th year German class is usually as far from
being the ideal end to a working day as I can think of, but it
is a positive relief after being alone in the smothering
presence of Judy Hartington for an hour. In this light, I
begin to look at these ugly brutes with something
approaching affection. They are ignorant and badly

behaved – no lesson with them contains enough silence for me to venture to do any oral questioning – but in a strange way they have grown on me. I tolerate their ways; my ambitions for them have been considerably lowered. As they read through an insultingly easy word search, I survey them as they work, savouring the comparative (and surely short-lived) silence and mood of industry.

There is the one they call Pooch. He is an unfeasibly tall and gangly youth, quite the most clumsy individual I have ever seen. He cannot walk past a desk without things falling off noisily. He is unfairly ugly, with a huge red nose and FA Cup ears at right angles to his spotty face. His black curly hair is reminiscent of that of a particularly unkempt poodle.

There is the one they call Chimp. His appearance is indeed Simian, his long arms dangle by his side as he lopes around the room. For Chimp follows you around the room. At my desk, as I open the blinds, as I scurry into the stock-cupboard, there is no rest from the determinedly ubiquitous Chimp. He cannot sit at his desk for more than a minute before getting up and walking around, which goes a long way towards explaining why he has never once done any written work whatsoever since September. He says, amicably enough: "I don't really do German."

There is the one they call Horny. He is fat with a freckle-ridden, permanently dirty face. Again, his shock of red hair seems to me to be the result of a rather unfair practical joke.

There are the Smith twins. Constantly on the move, constantly in trouble, they should be in the centre story of the Beano or Dandy, 'Those pesky Smith twits', or something similar. They have an old-fashioned look about them, are impeccably well-groomed, well-dressed, and are the most disruptive pupils in the room. One of them talks so much he is known as Yacker, but I am unable to work out which one.

134

The Mountain

There are the girls. They mostly sit sullenly on the back row, applying nail varnish and occasionally listening to personal stereos. I make no impact on them, I am beneath them. They are too pretty to have to do my work. The boys, too, are beneath them. While they compare burps and farts, the girls are in another world, quite possibly discussing tax-relief on mortgages and the pros and cons of income investment.

And there is Becky. She sits alone at the front. She looks up at me with those big cow eyes. They are watery with disappointment. She used to be my friend.

Now that I have been here for some time I am in the sights of Alan Evans, the deputy head, who also does the cover arrangements when staff are away. He says things like, "Now then, young man, I spared you for the first half-term, we don't use new teachers as much, but now you're one of us, you're one of the crew, so to speak, so you're fair game, ha, ha, I've got you in my sights, mind. You have more frees than most because you're new, and you could save us £20 or so on supply teachers, which we can't afford anyway, mind, so you're making your own little contribution to the financial well-being of the school, mind, I'm sure you won't be forgotten for it, ha, ha". I hate doing cover lessons even more than I hate my own. Today lesson 4 I am given a particularly gruesome looking 4th year Science group. They are already in the lab when I enter.

I approach the desk and try to look confident. This class does not know me, therefore will not know how easy it is to mess me around. They will treat me with the respect owed to an unknown quantity. I look down at the desk. There is no work attached to it.

"Settle down now, 4th years," I begin, my confidence ebbing with every second. "Where's the work?"

There is complete silence.

135

The Mountain

"Doesn't Miss Whiting attach work to the desk when she isn't here?"

A red-faced farmer boy wipes food away from his fat mouth and responds, with *faux* politeness:

"Sir, she never sets no work."

This gives confidence to a few others.

"Sir, she's never here, so how could she set work for not bein' here, if she's never here to set the work?" intones a tall horse-faced girl with at least three layers of make-up and improbably huge hooped earrings. The logic of her rhetorical question gains raucous applause from the others in the group, punctuated by generous spraying from the large taps on each bench, perhaps the collective equivalent of a formula one racing driver shaking up a champagne bottle on the victory podium.

As my luck would have it, Gillespie, my head of year and the nemesis of my credibility on more than one occasion this term, is also a Science teacher. He is also working in the prep-room next door. As he flings open the door I inwardly curse cheaply constructed schools with their complete lack of soundproofing.

"Account for this commotion!" he bellows, whereupon the class falls predictably silent. His rat-like eyes survey the scene, looking for the first sign of someone about to break the silence. His eyes finally rest on me.

"Ah, Mr Charon", he says in a friendly enough tone, yet one which seems at once to undermine me. He does not actually spell out the words 'now, that explains everything!' but he hardly needs to.

"Problem?" he asks, quietly and unnecessarily.

A small furtive looking boy who will probably be a police informer in a few years' time takes it upon himself to be my spokesman.

"Sir, sir can't find miss's work. It's not on the desk."

Gillespie wheels upon the grass, I fully expect the words 'who asked you to speak, boy?' but suddenly his

136

The Mountain

manner softens. He stands so close to the boy that they can
hear each other breathe, smiles eerily, and almost whispers:

"And why might that be, eh, Taylor? Why might
that be?"

The grass gulps. Gillespie wheels triumphantly
around towards the rest of the class in the manner of a
flamboyant public prosecutor about to put away a
defendant for five years. He is clearly enjoying his own
show.

"Why, I wonder, when Miss Whiting always
attaches her work to the desk, always, and I have worked
with her for ten years, why would she pick today of all
days to break with that particular habit? Hmm? Or could it
be that one of you…people…saw fit to remove it before Mr
Charon," – his eyes alight on mine, burning through them –
"actually…got here?"

The courtroom is spellbound; it is a charismatic
performance. But there is complete silence; this would be
an act of treachery too many, even for the future police
informer.

"Well then, I'll leave these worksheets on the
digestive system for you in Mr Charon's…capable hands.
Any trouble Mr Charon and…you know where I am."

This last statement is manifestly untrue, as
Gillespie heads for the door, not to the prep room, but to
the outside corridor, and disappears as suddenly as he
arrived. The 4th years and myself are relieved, but this
sudden solidarity is fleeting. Soon, there is no doubt about
who is on whose side.

"Sir, you gay?"

"'Course he ain't gay, he fancies Hartington!"

"That dog? 'Course he don't!"

"Yeah! I seen 'em! Talkin'!"

"She's a lezza!"

"Now settle down!" I shout. I am quite relieved;
for a moment I thought I was going to be dragged into the
conversation – 'Do you mind, I can answer for myself. No,

137

I don't fancy her. If you must know…' – and I am also pleasantly surprised that they have started to work on the worksheet.

It is a phoney peace which does not last. I make the fatal mistake of turning my back on the group. The noise of several light missiles hitting a hard surface force me to turn around abruptly, only to see a retaliation of a barrage of small hard sweets. I am not quite caught in the middle of this cross-fire, and although it ceases for a moment, I fear it is a battle I am losing.

I find listening to the conversations of those who are not involved in missile launching fascinating, much more interesting than the digestive system. A girl in the front row with teeth like tombstones and make-up like a call-girl in a 1970s porn movie says:

"Did a bong last night."

I look up but it is apparently not for my benefit. Her peroxide-blonde neighbour, on the other hand, appears riveted.

"Yeh! Me an' Jonno too. Where'd'you go?"

"Youth club bus shelter. Then we kicked it in, we pulled the whole lot down."

"Where'd'you get it?"

"Naylor. Nicked money from in here, Whiting's drawers. Always leaves them open."

"Whiting's drawers! Always open!! That old dog! Nahahaah!"

"I done a bong with Peanut."

"Oh yeah. Someone's done him over."

"Someone's done his car over."

"Yeh! An' him. Shaz were there."

"Shaz is a lez."

"Someone done him over."

"An' his car."

The seventies' street walker goes quiet and reflective.

The Mountain

The bell goes. No-one packs anything away. It is a race between me and them to get to the door. They win, but only just.

Coombs Park is the most dire hovel I have ever seen in my life. The approach heralds the deprivation and the hopelessness within. I walk up a mud-sodden path, the rain constantly nagging at my face. I pass skips full of car exhausts, heavy duty cable, rusted prams, empty barrels of oil and burned out cars flank either side of the path. A child's bicycle frame lies broken to one side, complete with a row of the fencing to which it presumably was once locked. A group of skin-headed, tattooed youths stand in a cluster smoking and eye me with tangible suspicion, their beady eyes flickering nastily as they watch me approach the first caravans.

I obtained Anna's address from the school secretary, and I glance nervously at the scrap of paper I noted it down on: '10 Ash Drive, Coombs Holiday Park'. Some town planner or holiday park developer has a rich vein of ironic humour. Number 10 is further up the hill, past a collection of ramshackle caravans and some discarded tractor tyres. Somewhere someone is making a chemical bonfire, the main ingredient of which seems to be rubber, and a filthy black smoke hangs heavily in the air. Hungry looking dogs wander aimlessly about barking and whining as they scavenge in bins.   Number 10 is perched precariously at the top of a hill.

The door is unlocked. I venture inside – the room smells of stale neglect. Clothes lie in a huddle on the floor, a broken window has been temporarily mended with tape, dirty plates and cups form a pile of the table, the only real item of furniture. Schoolbooks strewn around the floor are the only evidence that children of a school age once inhabited this shack, I can find nothing here to help me in my search for Anna. Has she returned here? In all

139

probability not, the authorities would have sought her here immediately. I rustle through some papers left on the table – a betting slip, an old newspaper, a shopping list – I feel curiously like a burglar as I read through the contents. There is nothing for me here, it was a mistake to come, and I leave the caravan with a strong sense of relief.

Lou is sitting in my flat later that evening and is trying to sing. He opines that at first there seems to have been a mountain, then is less sure, then confirms his original impression, logically if slightly tunelessly. For my benefit, he has come round to my flat with his battered guitar and a minstrel's supply of sundry songs. I am too polite to tell him that this is not the ideal night for his musings on the presence of mountains. I am reluctant to say something that might offend him. In fact, given how much I champion the truth and plain speaking on behalf of other people, I am remarkably cowardly when it comes to me speaking the truth to other people. Our dialogue unfolds like this:

"Donovan. He's the man. Am I bugging you, a redundant presence?"

"What?"

"Am I… redundant? Is there a point in my being here?"

"I don't mind."

"I got the vibe before that you might want to be alone."

"No, I'm OK really." And I can hear myself saying it - it comes out automatically, this practised hypocrisy. And my chance has gone.

"There's something really sad about last night's ashes."

"What?"

The Mountain

"Last night's ashes, you know like, last night's fire. We had a fire in here last night, now the ashes are all that remain. Cold, white grey. Dead."

"Oh."

Lou has not finished.

"Where once there was life. So much life. I find it sad. And empty."

The conversation continues like this for an indeterminate length of time. It could be hours, or I could glance at my watch and see that it has been two minutes. Suddenly the doorbell rings. The interruption is welcome, until I open the door. It is Judy.

"Hello. Just popped in, thought we might have some…fun together," she coos in an irritatingly sunny manner combined with her idea of a seductive pause thrown in at the end. Amazingly, Lou takes the hint.

"Gotta split. Too heavy. Things to do."

I want to shake Lou. Minutes ago, I wanted to hit him hard, to curse his cod-hippy warblings about whether he knew if there was a mountain or not. Now I want to hug him as well, and whisper to him that he is my dearest friend, he need not split, it is not in the least bit heavy and it is very unlikely that he has anything at all to do. I want to share more of his conversation, all evening long if need be. But he vanishes into the wet night.

I sit down on the sofa. Judy wastes no time in sitting on top of me.

"Sleep with me," she says (again).

It is time for my dishonest dissembling to stop. I make a deep sigh to buy me some more time.

"I'm sorry, Judy. I can't."

"Why not? What do you mean?"

"I just…can't."

"Tired after last night, I suppose."

I nearly fall for it. The old me would have said 'yes', and taken the consequences.

"No, it's not that."

141

The Mountain

"What is it, then?"

I sigh again.

"I don't really want to."

Judy's face is quite red, and her manner has changed.

"What? Why not? You wanted to enough last night!"

"Yes, but-"

"But what?"

"All right then, no!"

"No what?"

"No, I didn't want to last night. At least, not particularly."

"Then, why did you?"

"You told me to."

"What?"

"You told me to. You practically forced me to. Just like you tried to do just now."

Judy is not just pretending, she is truly indignant. Her emotions may be plastic affectations most of the time, but this is for real.

"You didn't seem to mind too much at the time," she sniffs.

"Well, no, I didn't, I mean, I don't. It's just that-"

"That what? What's so different?"

"I don't know." This will hurt. "The cold light of day, I guess."

"The what? How dare you! You used me when I was drunk. Now you're sober you just want to dump me. You bastard!"

"Judy, it's not like that," I say weakly. "I just don't want to get involved."

"Well you *are* involved," she snaps. "Trust me, you do *not* want to have me as an enemy."

It sounds as if she is perhaps throwing me a last-minute lifeline, a chance to lie again. But she is not, she is too hurt for that, and she picks up her handbag and goes.

The Mountain

I should feel relieved. I have bitten the bullet and told the ugly truth. Instead I feel cheap, shabby and empty, and that wretched emotion pity takes hold. I feel sorry for Judy, and want to run after her and see if she is all right. But in the words that could be from one of Lou's aphorisms, what has been said cannot be unsaid. I gaze emptily into the ashes of last night's fire

Chapter 14

From the second my feet hit the ground I'm runnin'. I jump the last few rungs of the fire escape ladder an' run off into the night. I know what I'm doin' alright. If I'm to get home at all it has to be now, before they notice I'm gone. Home is the first place they'd look for me, even the coppers could work out that I'd go home at some stage. So it has to be now.

It's exactly two miles from the social worker's poxy house to home, I've run it before. But now I really have to leg it, if they see I'm gone they'll call the pigs in no time. That nosy bastard Osborne only followed me up to the loo, he'll find out within five minutes at the most. I can do this run in fifteen minutes flat if I really push myself. That gives him ten minutes to contact the pigs and for them to get out to the Park – I should be OK, but I've really got to leg it.

I hated it in there. It'll do Darren's head in when he finds I'm gone, but it's for the best. I'll find Dad myself, then they'll let Darren out an' we can all move back into the caravan again. It's not much, it's not anything really, but it is our home. The social worker's place was really doin' my head in. It's the kind of place where they say "that's just the way it is" the whole time. When they can't think of an answer, or can't be bothered reasonin' with you, or if you ask too awkward questions, that's their standard answer. "Why do we have to be in here?" – "That's just the way it is." "Why can't I see Darren?" – "That's just the way it is." "Why can't I go back to my home?" – "That's just the way it is." I had that

144

The Mountain

at school the whole time too, especially from Gillespie.
"Why do we have to wear this skanky uniform?" – "That's
just the way it is." "Why can't I have music lessons?" –
"That's just the way it is." "Why am I being excluded,
when she hit me first?" – "That's just the way it is." All
my scuffin' life people have fobbed me off with "that's just
the way it is" and no-one can explain why.

I do the first mile in seven minutes twenty
seconds, so I'm on target, just. The second mile is uphill,
very steep, so I need to leg it. I should be OK. I can do the
half marathon course around here in one hour forty, which
is almost exactly seven and a half minute miles, in fact I
would nearly win the women's race with that time if I
could be bothered to enter it, which I can't. But this is
important now, so even without my proper running shoes I
have to match my quickest time. Up by the railings that
mark the edge of town, across a muddy field which slows
me down but is a bit quicker-and safer-than the main road,
past the bins and broken-down lorries and I'm at the edge
of the park. Only a few hundred metres now, but I have to
sprint, they'll be on to me. A quick burst up the hill, my
lungs feel they want to explode. I'm dizzy and feel sick.
But I'm running for my freedom, I won't stop. I make it in
fourteen minutes twenty-five seconds.

Into the caravan, home at last. No sign of Dad.
Not even a scabby note. I rifle through his things. His
wallet's gone, so's his coat, but that don't tell me much.
He could be down the legion. I want to leave a note, but
any help I give the pigs in tracing me is too much help,
even though if they had a brain they'd know I'd come here
first. Back down the hill then, but this time I gotta be even
more careful.

Sure enough, there's a pig car pullin' up at the
bottom of the park as I leave, with a pig-dog yappin' its
thick head off. No way I can go down that way, I'll have to
escape by the top end of the park and run round. That's a
distance of about an extra mile but it's the only way to go,

so I leg it like mad and head for the fence at the top end. I can hear the pigs an' their stupid dogs in the background, hope they don't shine a torch at me, and I'm leggin' it towards the fence.

I knew I'd have to climb the fence, but it's taken me by surprise, I haven't been up this way for ages. It's two metres high, someone's mended the big hole in it and there's barbed wire at the top. Still, I've got to do it, so I climb up and grab on to the barbed wire, cuttin' my hands all over the place. Then I'm vaultin' over it, can't see where I land but I know to keep runnin', round the outside of the park, where the pig-dogs won't see me and can't reach me anyway, down to the legion.

'Course outside the legion I have to put up with the usual dirty old piss-heads, wanting to finger me an' that. I'm desperate, I'm like, "Me dad been in?" an' they're like, "Ooh, you're looking gorgeous this evening." I'm not, I look a state, in my mad rush I didn't pick up any clean clothes at home and I'm covered in sweat and blood. I can't take any more waiting so I burst in the door, but he's not there.

That leaves the Lion, the only pub in this godforsaken dump that's sure to serve him. To get there I have to go through the centre of the town, there's no other way, but with any luck the pigs will still be staggering around the Park in their confusion. Even so I gotta be quick, it's mostly downhill so I sprint. The Lion is a horrible modern building, looks like a big public loo, and the people are yobbier than at the legion, it's dog-rough and normally I wouldn't go near it. Some kids are playing in the entrance and there's a girl with a baby in a pram, probably minding the brat while the parents are inside getting rat-arsed. I push past them. Inside a telly is blaring, it's all neon lights and it smells of piss and disinfectant. Some old tramp is sitting at the bar talking to himself, a bag-lady is playin' some card game with her skanky daughter and some boy-racers are crowded round

146

The Mountain

the fruit machine. Otherwise the place is empty, so I go up
to the bar, I goes, "Me dad been in? Arthur Lomas." The
tramp stops talking to himself and seems to sit up and take
notice, but he seems so mad you can't trust that. Anyway
the fat slob of a barman goes, "No, haven't seen him in
days." He seems to know this is bad news, worse than him
just goin' missin' for the night, or maybe it's the state I'm
in or something, 'cos he reaches under the bar and reaches
me a stale looking cheese cob. "Here, duck, get this down
your neck," he goes, the fat patronising git.

I'm cold, it's raining, I'm knackered, I'm covered
in blood, I'm apart from Dad and Darren and don't dare see
Tracey or Becky and the pigs are searchin' for me, and all
I've got's this one bloody stale cheese cob. That's just the
way it is.

The one person I could get in touch with is
Charon. Then at least I'd know if he cared. It goes
through my mind, as I dart in and out of the shadows,
hiding from every car that comes my way. It could work –
people wouldn't suspect him of sheltering me; Tracey and
Becky might, but they wouldn't dob. I could get him to
pass on the message that I'm OK. But I don't know where
he lives. It's well too dodgy to go up to school to meet him
there. School would be the second place the pigs and their
dogs would look.

I'm stuck. I can't contact anyone, can't go to the
park, and can't find Dad, which was the point of me
escaping. I'm desperate, so I decide on something I've
never done before.

There's an old house just the other side of town,
just to the south – me and my mates used to play there as
kids, in the days when we had a proper house and when I
had mates. It's like an old hotel type place, been empty for
years. When we played in the grounds it was in a bad state,
outside anyway, and they talked about doing it up properly

but nothing happened. It's in an even worse mess now. I head out on the country road that leads to it, at least no pig-car will follow me out here, it's the back of beyond. I'm there in ten minutes, and it's still there, all boarded up. I sneak round the back and pull away the chipboard from one of the windows. I pull myself up with what remaining strength I've got and I'm inside.

Inside it's cold, it stinks and of course it's completely dark. I feel my way past some tables, there's rubble, bricks and broken glass all over the floor. I fumble in the dark for a clear bit of floor, just so I can lie on it. It's horrible, it's spooky and I swear I can hear rats scufflin' about. But it's dry, the pigs won't find me, so I'll stay here for a while, just until I get my head together.

I've no idea how long I slept. I didn't think I would, it was so cold and horrible, but I was so knackered I just must have dosed off. It's light when I next open my eyes, anyway. Sort of. Everything's boarded up so there isn't much light. I see loads of tables, workmen's tools and benches, and not much more. There's a pad and a pencil. I get a brainwave. I write a message to Charon, like, you've gotta help me, meet me in the Park at 6 tomorrow night, and I'll get Becky to give it to him, I'll get her on her way to school. And then I think: this is really risky. I'm trembling all over just thinkin' about it, although the cold doesn't exactly help. What if they're watching Becky's every step, knowing that I'd try to get in touch? I could hide in bushes and jump out at her, but what if they were following her? I don't dare go up to school, no way. And there's no-one I trust enough to pass on a message, just Becky an' Tracey, but the pigs'll be watching them. And do I trust Charon? And if we meet in the Park, will they be looking for us there?

So I think some more. Today's only Monday, the first school day after Guy Fawkes Day; they'll be looking

148

everywhere for me and going through the school and
leisure centre areas, as well as spying on my only two
mates. There's nothing for it but to wait a bit. If I wait 'till
say, Wednesday, that should give things time to settle a bit
and there may not be so many pigs everywhere.

It's cold and I'm hungry, but I gotta stay for at
least a couple of days. I'm bored and miserable, my whole
body aches. Then on the table I see the outline of a tube of
glue. It'll be ancient but it might still work, the tube's not
been opened. I use a knackered old pair of pliers to open
the lid, and I'm so desperate I shove the nozzle straight up
one nostril, no plastic bag or anything, then up the other
one, deep, deep breath. Once again, each nostril. It doesn't
feel too good, but my head is spinning, I've forgotten how
hungry I was and I feel all numb. That'll have to do for
now.

I stumble around in the half-darkness, tripping
over stuff on the floor. I find the note-pad and I begin to
write:

'Dear Charon,

If you ever cared anything about me, meet me
again in the park, at 6, on Wednesday. Whatever you do
don't tell anyone. I need you desperately.

A.'

I just get it written then my head feels well heavy,
like it doesn't belong to me but it's throbbing. I feel tingly
with pins and needles all over and sick. Not just my head
but my whole body seems to be spinning, and I just want it
to stop. I just want everything to stop. I want so many
things that I can't have, and I don't know why I can't have
them. I want Ed, I want Mum, I want Darren, and I never
ever thought I'd say this, but I want Dad back. I'm tired
and hungry and fed up and I don't know why I can never
ever get the things I want.

Chapter 15

When I go to open the staffroom door Tracey and Becky are there again; this is getting to be a habit. They don't talk, their faces betray no forgiveness, just Becky stares up at me with her big watery eyes. And she hands me a note. They disappear as I open it, they don't wait to see what trust I am about to break, they don't want to be seen near me. On balance that has to be a good thing, but I want to shout out after them "Wait! You can trust me! You can!"

My fingers tremble as I unfold the note, because I know who the author is. She reveals nothing of her whereabouts but wants to meet me again in the Park. I am astonished, as our only other meeting was a complete disaster. We have still barely spoken to each other. What have I suddenly done to gain her trust?

It all happened with horrific suddenness. Gianluca and Paolo, down by the river. And Marcia and me – I was her boyfriend now, I was family. And no-one was angry with me. The river Arly glistened madly in the darkness, a river of quicksilver dancing amongst the heavy pebbles. We looked down from the bridge, the family. And not one of us heard them coming.

Gianluca had arranged to meet Paolo, to confront him with the enormity of his crime. Marcia was to be the exhibit, I would be there as the voice of reason, the force of good. We would then leave Gianluca to exact his revenge, witnessed only by the cold waters and the stern mountains.

The Mountain

A single rifle shot pierced the thin air, cracked like a bone being broken. As one we turned to see a red truck turn in the dirt road, raising clouds of dust as it accelerated into the night. And we didn't even see, or hear. Gianluca lurched silently towards Marcia, she held her big brother in her arms for a second, and we saw what was there – a large patch of deep crimson blood disfiguring the back of his head, a red hole, blood trickling down the back of his neck and onto Marcia's white dress, darting here and there like the waters of the river. Gianluca shot in the back of the head by a single blow from a rifle, Paolo, 'l'homme à la carabine' and his henchmen had spoiled the revenge party. And Marcia, distraught, disfigured by her brother's blood, struggled to hold his weight, and Gianluca's broken body fell off the bridge and into the river of mercury.

I stood perfectly helplessly. The family's blood had been shed. And still no-one was angry with me.

Judy and Eleanor are talking to Geoff in the staffroom. I join their table out of habit, but the atmosphere is distinctly cool. Judy will not look me in the eye. Eleanor is talking to Geoff about cars.

"Oh, Geoff, that would be so handy, you're a darling. When could you service it?"

"This weekend? Sunday?"

"Oh, that would be amazing?"

"It's only a service."

Judy joins the conversation.

"Geoff, can you do brakes?"

"Do what to them?"

"I don't know, they're squeaking or something. Frances says they're pulling a bit, but he's bloody useless." She looks furtively at me. "I seem destined to be surrounded by useless men, so this makes a nice change, Geoff. If you could look at them?"

The Mountain

"Sounds like the pads are worn. What car?"

"You know, the four by four. Daihatsu. With the animal on the spare tyre."

"Pop it round on Sunday," says the only non-useless man in Judy's circle of acquaintances.

"So, Frances is useless, you must be useless, not bad going!" he says to me in a bid to lighten the atmosphere.

"But you're OK."

"I'm OK, apparently. What about the others, I wonder? What about David, with his long sentences and his Latin? What about Lou?"

"Lou's bloody useless. He can't even decide if there's a mountain or not."

"What?"

"Just something he said."

"He says some things," David agrees.

She needs me desperately. The tone of Anna's letter is different, I feel, from the last one. Will the tone of our meeting be different?

I arrive at the park slightly before six. The scene is as gloomy as it was last time, the ever-present rain makes my clothes stick to me. I am cold and uncomfortable, but feel strangely needed. I hear a rustle from amongst some bushes and a drenched, lugubrious figure emerges. It is Anna.

I strain my eyes to make sure it is her. She is soaking and shivering uncontrollably. Her hands and face have mud and blood on them and the dark rings around her eyes, even in this bad light, give her the appearance of a destitute sunken-eyed drug addict. She is emaciated and crouched down as though in fear.

"Anna? Is that you?"

None of the hostility of our last meeting seems present, even at this early stage. Whatever the fight was, she seems to have given it up. She approaches me nervously.

The Mountain

"They're after me." This is one of the longest sentences she has spoken to me, ever.

"Who are? Who's they?"

"Them. Everyone."

"What are you talking about?"

"Can you just…take me somewhere…safe?" She seems on the verge of collapse.

"Where? You've got to explain?"

"Later. Quick, they're after me."

"Who?"

"Pigs."

I want to put my arms around her. I want to protect her. Her confusion and paranoia seem intense. She is also freezing and starving so I must act without delay.

"OK, listen. I'll take you to my flat, you can at least get warmed up. I'll get you something to eat. You can have a wash. We can cut through the Park. If we stay close to the bushes and trees, no-one will see us. My flat's just at the other side."

She follows eagerly, grateful like a wild animal being offered a reprieve from the hunt. She follows me in silence. At the flat she lurks nervously outside, hesitant in the glare of the street lights yet unsure as to whether it is appropriate for her to enter.

"Go on in, you go ahead, it's OK."

My flat has never been tidy but even with its array of bottles and clothing strewn all over every available surface it must seem the ultimate in luxurious domesticity compared to her caravan, far less wherever she has been staying for the past few nights.

"Nice." She looks around suspiciously. "Tidy."

Although I know nothing about her, I am surprised at the resilience that allows a flicker of a sense of humour to peek through all that gloom.

"It's home," I say, and then immediately wish I hadn't. I am trying not to be too paternal, too cloyingly protective and to remain nothing like those authority

153

figures she has encountered so far in her life and whom she so deeply mistrusts. It is a difficult balancing act.

"How about a hot bath," I suggest benevolently, "followed by something to eat and drink, then you can begin to tell me what's going on."

She hesitates.

"Can I stay?" A couple of weeks ago I might have kissed her for asking the question; now, I'm really not sure. But I do so want her trust.

"We'll see. For tonight maybe. But you're going to have to go back sometime. People are worried about you." I stop there. That's enough of the responsible caring adult. She needs a bath more than she needs my empty words.

I too am soaked through, so I empty my pockets onto the kitchen table and go to get changed. I sort out some old clothes that Anna can wear a shapeless old sweatshirt and tracksuit trousers. My reputation in the kitchen is only slightly superior to that deserved by my general housekeeping skills, but I try to concoct a hot soup (from a tin) which in films would be what they offered a similarly bedraggled foundling. I turn up the heating and try to make Anna's temporary accommodation as welcoming as possible.

Anna emerges from the bath completely covered in two large towels, and sees the clothes I have thoughtfully placed for her by the door.

"Nice," she says again.

"It's not high fashion." I begin, in a weak attempt at levity, "but it's something warm and dry." I make myself cringe. The more I think about it, the more I become convinced that it would be better if I didn't talk at all.

I leave Anna to don my baggy garments and busy myself by fretting over the soup. She enters the kitchen a few minutes later, looking like a particularly mournful clown in my ill-fitting clothes.

154

The Mountain

"That looks better," I lie.

"It'll do."

"I'm a bit bigger than you are around the waist."

"Look, Charon," she says, obviously tired at my feeble attempts at light conversation, "thanks for putting me up. I just need some rest, some food, a chance to get my head together, then I'm gone, I promise. I won't be a burden to you."

"You can stay," I reason with her, although these are not the wisest words I could have chosen.

"No. But I gotta trust you. Tell no-one I'm here. Not even after I'm gone."

"Strictly speaking, after you're gone, you'll no longer be here."

"You know what I mean. Promise."

"OK. Promise."

"I trust you."

"You can."

"You don't understand. I trust no-one, usually. But I need you. I need someone to trust. It's tiring not having anyone to trust, it's doing me head in. I'm tired of running and I'm tired of not trusting. You gotta promise."

For all I know this is the longest speech she has ever made in her life - there are certainly more words in it than I have ever heard her utter. It is plainly heartfelt; she seems close to tears.

"I promise." My words are so empty, so unconvincing beside hers.

"If I get caught, they'll stick me in another home, a worse one. I'll never see Darren again, or Dad. You'll get sacked. Can you see how important this is?"

"Yes. You can trust me. I promise."

Her relief is almost tangible. She is tired of not trusting, and for now, it seems, this burden has been lifted. She smiles, closes her eyes, and leans across the kitchen table and kisses me on the forehead.

155

The Mountain

We sit. We don't chat any longer. The soup thing happens, more or less, and then we just sit. There is a serenity about our silence, however, which I quite like. The room is peaceful.

"That's better," she says after a while. "Can I sleep somewhere?"

"You must be tired. Take my bed."

"You sure?"

"Sure. I'm quite used to the sofa, anyway."

"Thanks. I'm grateful. I trust you."

With that, she's gone.

I feel that I've done something useful, and I'm strangely moved. I'm drawn to Anna, I definitely like her, and I could almost discern some warmth in her for the first time. I don't know what the future holds, but for now things are working out. The best would be for her to stay here tonight, to get warmed up and fed and to have a decent night's sleep, then to hand herself in. I feel exhausted, but that must be nothing to how she feels. It's only 9 o'clock but it feels much later; we've been through the equivalent of two or three evenings since 6. I browse in the fridge for a well-earned beer. Anna will be asleep next door. At the exact moment I open the can, the door-bell rings. My heart stops.

I open the door and see a very sodden Judy.

"Judy," I say.

"Well spotted."

"You're soaking."

"Nothing gets past you, Nigel."

In a film, at this point I would say, reluctantly, 'you'd better come in then.' It is the half-hearted invitation reserved for unwanted and unannounced guests. A brief and cold exchange would ensue. The unwanted guest would then leave in a hurry, saying something like 'don't worry, I'll see myself out'. But Judy doesn't wait; she sees herself in.

"You do."

156

The Mountain

"What?"

"You get past me."

"What?"

"You said 'nothing gets past you'. But, you see, you just have."

"Nigel for God's sake! This is serious. I'm not in a mood for your stupid word games."

She's right, although without knowing why. A runaway 15-year-old pupil is in my bed, the person I least want to see in the entire world has just walked into my kitchen, and I'm making puns.

"So, d'you want a drink?"

"A big one."

"That sounds ominous." I make her a large gin with a little tonic. "What's so urgent?"

"Oh, well, it's nice to see *you,* too," she replies with unnecessarily laboured sarcasm.

"Sorry."

She takes a very large swig from the glass, nearly emptying it, and sighs theatrically.

"If you *must* know…" Her voice trails off.

"I wouldn't say 'must'. I'm interested of course. But 'must'…"

"For Christ's sake Nigel!! Stop it!"

She has a point. I am even irritating myself.

"Sorry," I say again. "Do tell."

"Well, if you *must* know, I think Frances suspects."

"Suspects what?"

"Whom. Suspects us."

"Us?" I am flabbergasted. "There is no us."

"Oh, but there is," she counters wisely as she empties her glass. "And my Frances suspects."

I refill her glass and open another beer.

"Explain."

"Last week when I slept over." I shudder.

157

The Mountain

"You said – but - he had a Masons' meeting, or something-"

"He did."

"I thought he stayed out half the night drinking on those occasions. I thought you said he wouldn't even notice if you were there or not."

"You thought, you thought. You do a lot of thinking. It just so happens that that particular meeting ended early. His main drinking mates went on to another function, God knows why but Frances decided not to join them. Something about not much liking the chap at whose house it was, or something."

"I see."

"So he was home by 10 that evening, wondering where the hell I was."

"And what did you tell him?"

"That I was at Eleanor's, that I had too much drink so had to crash out at hers."

"That at least sounds plausible."

"It would have worked too, but this evening – he met us both in town at the Wine Bar before his Rotarians' meeting – Eleanor stared blankly at him when he asked if the two of us had sobered up since last week. She couldn't remember me sleeping at hers, until I kicked her hard under the table."

"And?"

"Well, he's not completely stupid. We've been here before. He didn't want to make a scene in the Wine Bar, but I'm dreading going back home. He knows who was there that night, I'd already told him, so he may put two and two together."

"So you came round here this evening. Good thinking."

"Nigel, we have to talk. We have to sort out a story."

"Why me? I wasn't the only bloke there."

The Mountain

"For Christ's sake! Can you imagine me with David or Geoff? Do you think he can? Or with fake-hippy Lou. Come *on*!"

"I'm flattered."

"Well stop being. Think of a story."

"You were really drunk. Slept on the sofa. That's all."

"Oh, Nigel," she sighs, as if I had just explained to her the laws of nuclear fission. "You make it sound so…simple."

Judy can change from hard-nosed interrogator from hell into little girl lost in seconds and it is very disarming. She is in this latter mode as she sidles up to me on my kitchen chair which barely has room for one.

"Oh, Nigel, you're so clever," she simpers as she caresses my hair.

"That must be the gin talking, but which one?"

"Where would I be without you?" She strokes my arm.

"Not in this mess, anyway."

She won't be put off.

"Frances' meeting doesn't end for another half hour or so. I'm meeting him at home, so we have…time, you and I."

"Are you quite mad?" It isn't the most winning of chat-up lines, but it strikes me as being close to the mark.

"Mad for you! Nigel, I'm 34 years old, I haven't had much of a life, I'm married to a drunken Tory pig and I want some adventure; I deserve some. If I'm going to get found out, I may as well make it worthwhile. I have fond memories of through there." With that she beckons unmistakeably towards my bedroom door. I gulp.

"Um, no, Judy, that really won't work."

"Oh, Nigel, I'm dying for you."

"No."

"Oh, come on, just this once. I'll go and get myself ready, you come in in a minute."

The Mountain

"Judy, that's not going to happen."

Her face hardens; she can change back moods in an instant, too.

"Right, if that's the way you want it!"

"It is."

"You don't want to cross me, Nigel!" She is angry and emotional; I sit calmly and watch her as she sweeps up her handbag and car keys from the debris on the kitchen table. At 9.30 exactly, she is gone.

Chapter 16

The alarm on my watch goes at 5.30 am. Not much point, really. I can't sleep in this hole. Although it's dark 'till quite late these mornings, I ain't takin' no chances. Pigs an' social do-gooders will still be lookin' for me, especially near school. I have worked out a plan. After all, I've had plenty of time cooped up in this hole for the last couple of days. It's time to put my plan into action.

I make for the window frame I climbed in through however many days ago it was, and climb out of it. Simple enough, but I ain't takin' no chances. If those bastards catch me they'll lock me up for good. So I keep in the shadows, round the back of the building and follow my tracks back into town. With it being so dark, at least I can see any vehicle coming for miles and hide in the shadows if I need to. That's what my life has been, these last few days – hidin' in the shadows.

I stink – I mean *really* stink. I stink of cold clammy sweat and of a dirty, dusty old house. My breath stinks like it does when you haven't eaten or slept for days. I'm cold and wet and shivering the whole time, even when I break into a run for a bit I'm still shiverin' an' frozen. Plus, I'm too knackered to run. And in my mind I'm askin' myself how it got to this, why am I here, what am I doin' out here in the cold at 5.30 am? A milk float drives by, and almost out of habit I hide behind some bushes.

It's only November but it's freezin'. I'm nearing the town now, so gotta be really careful. Gotta be ready to

The Mountain

run, too, although it's the last thing I feel like doin'. I take
the long way round, sticking to the outskirts, it's a really
long walk up to school this way then I'm heading past it,
out the other side. There is some traffic around now, so
I'm slowed down by hiding in every second house's drive
'till the roads are clear, just in case.

After about forty-five minutes I reach Curbar
Avenue, a big snob street to the north of town. It's quite a
way out, the opposite direction to where I've been staying,
and it's on Becky's way to school. It's 7.15. I have a good
hour to wait. I walk up and down the road until I find a
good garden or drive to hide in. That's the good thing
about these big snob houses. The gardens are so massive,
with their bushes and patios and conservatories that the
drives are about half a mile from the front doors of the
houses. About half way down on the left is a huge one
we've hidden in before, to have an early morning smoke or
sniff of something out of the reaches of the neighbourhood
watch scheme and their pissy prying eyes. No 35,
'Castlemount'. Leilandia and beech trees make a nice
screen for a girl to hide in. I find a dry spot in amongst a
kind of shrubbery and wait. Hope they don't have a dog.

I know Becky's way to school off by heart. She's
the nearest thing to a best friend that I've ever had, apart
from Ed anyway, and a creature of habit. We often used to
walk to school together, anyway. It's not especially my
way – I live, or lived, more sort of northwest of town, this
is northeast – but we'd often meet up and have a fag and a
laugh. I treasured those laughs, as I knew that fairly often
it would be the last laugh I'd have all day.

So anyway, the plan's a good one. Becky'll be
along here about 8.15, alone, I'll chuck a stone at her,
she'll come into the drive, I'll pass her the note. Nothing
can go wrong. Then it hits me – I've left the note back at
the house I was hiding in.

Now it's high risk stuff, 'cos I'm gonna have to
talk to Becky while I write the note again. The chances of

162

The Mountain

us being seen together have increased. But it's my only
chance, so I might as well go for it. The sun is trying to
come up, and the time is passing really slowly. Towards 8
o'clock, I'm gettin' well nervous. Some spotty little brats
pass me on their way to school, unbearable little creeps
who actually want to be early. A fat little 1st year on his
poxy bike wobbles up the drive on his paper round. The
milkman and postman come and go. A Volvo comes down
the drive, followed by a Range Rover – I do believe the
master and lady of the house are leaving. One bumper
sticker says 'Cheshire stockbrokers do it standing up with
their arms waving about', whilst the one on the Range
Rover says '*I* slow down for horses'.

It's 8.10. Now loads of people are around – cars,
dog-walkers, old ladies, several pupils. I'm gonna have to
be well careful here. I get out of the shrubs and sneak
towards the end of the drive. I stick my neck out and look
to the right. And there, in the distance, is Becky's
unmistakeable shape. I want to run out and kiss her.

Instead, I wait patiently. She's slow, but she's a
big girl. And bang on 8.15, she passes the end of the drive.
I wait 'till she passes and lob a clump of earth at her,
whack! It hits her on the back of the neck! She turns
round, looking angry and confused, 'till I goes "Oy, Beck!
Here!" She still looks confused, I don't blame her.

"Oy!"
"Who's that?"
"Me! Get in here!"
"Anna?"
"Get in here, now!"
"Did you peg that mud at me?"
"Get here, *now!!*"

I think she knows it's pretty serious. She moves
quickly, we're both in the drive amongst the poncey bushes
that you have when you're a Cheshire stockbroker. And
she's like, "Omigod! Look at the state of you!"

163

The Mountain

I goes, "So? You're not exactly Miss Beautiful," which is cheap and crap and I hate myself for it. She's like, "Where you been? We've been worried sick!"

"I gotta trust you."

"'Course."

"I'll be back soon."

"Good. We miss you."

"I need to write a note. Give me a pen and paper."

Becky's not that quick anyway. Now I'm only asking for the two least likely things to be found in her school bag. If I'd said, 'Fags? Make-up?' no problem. But a pen, in Becky's bag? Paper?

"Quick!" I snap.

"Calm down!"

After what seems ages she finds them. I scrawl out the same message to Charon, I've learned it by heart.

"Take that to Charon."

"That git?"

"Please." It's the first time I've used the word.

"Why?"

"Listen Becky," I goes. I'm in real trouble. You can't be seen talkin' to me. Give this to Charon. I'll be in touch. Now go."

She goes, poor cow. I want to yell after her, 'Please! I miss you too!' I want to yell, 'say 'hi' to Tracey'. I can't. I hope Becky understands that I can't.

My mission is completed, however. I may as well stay in my Castlemount. Looking around the garden, I spot a shed hidden away in a corner. It's a bit small and skanky, probably not even their second or third choice shed, but that has its advantages 'cos the thing isn't even locked. Inside there's a few manky old tools and gardener type stuff, but it's dry and a lot warmer that outside. There's an old rug on the floor and I curl up on it, and within minutes I'm almost asleep. I have to laugh at the thought that these people's fourth choice shed or whatever is a whole lot

164

better than where I've been sleeping these last few nights. I'd laugh if it weren't so sad.

The day passes somehow. There's not exactly a lot to do here, it's a shed. But I sleep a bit. I sleep as much as I can to stop the hunger and boredom. If I'd thought, I'd have asked Becky to bring me some food. Another order here or there won't make no difference. I daren't go out and nick something, I'd get seen. As it is I'm gonna have fun getting down to the Park at 6 to meet Charon.

At 4 I hear the schoolkids on their way back home. I don't dare go out and see if Becky's there, I can't risk it. On the other hand I'd best be gone from here before 5. Posh streets, or avenues, probably don't have anything as common as a rush hour, but I can't risk being seen, and I sure as hell don't wanna be here when the Cheshire set get back from wherever the hell they pretend to work. At about quarter to 4.45 I start to make a move. It's not exactly dark but fortunately for me it's foggy. That and the rain mean there's not too many people around, so I make it to the Park without getting taken into custody.

I hide in some bushes 'till about 6. I'm getting used to these bushes. These ones aren't dry, though, they're cold and wet. I preferred the posh people's bushes. Suddenly through the fog, I just about make out a shape.

"Anna? Is that you?"

It's Charon. I hope he's not as useless as the last time we met. This time, I'm well desperate. I'm well nervous, too, but I goes up to him. I goes, "They're after me."

"Who are? Who's they?"

"Them. Everyone."

"What are you talking about?"

"Can you just…take me somewhere…safe?" I'm cold, hungry and knackered, and really desperate, otherwise I'd never have asked.

"Where? You've got to explain?"

"Later. Quick, they're after me."

165

The Mountain

"Who?"

"Pigs."

He seems to be listening. This might work. Surely he won't dob me. This is a risk, but I ain't got no choice. I'm freezing and starving.

"OK, listen. I'll take you to my flat, you can at least get warmed up. I'll get you something to eat. You can have a wash. We can cut through the Park. If we stay close to the bushes and trees, no-one will see us. My flat's just at the other side."

I want to throw my arms around him. I didn't really think he'd be this helpful. I can forgive him anything. We get to the flat in a couple of minutes.

"Go on in, you go ahead, it's OK."

So here we are, at last. After what seems like weeks of dossing down in places I don't want to be in, at last this feels like somewhere I want to be. It's not great, but I feel safe here. It's home, at least for a little while, at least I hope.

Charon's flat's a tip, a right dump. I didn't think anything was worse than our caravan, until I went to the social workers' place. Then the abandoned house. OK, Charon's pad isn't quite that bad, but it makes our caravan seem almost tidy. Beer bottles, papers, food stuff piled high all over the place. I've often wondered what they meant by bachelor flats.

I goes, "Nice. Tidy." I feel a bit bad, though, 'cos he has put himself out to help me this time.

He's like, "It's home." Strange thing to say. Strange idea, that, home. Then he's like, all paternal and that, which I can well do without but it is quite nice that he cares. He's like, "How about a hot bath," and all that old fogey type stuff, which normally I'd well hate but I gotta admit just for one night I could sink into, and go along with their ideas of home comfort. Now he's milkin' it, though, he's like, "followed by something to eat and drink, then you can begin to tell me what's going on."

166

The Mountain

I hesitates. I goes,"Can I stay?" I need to trust him.

"We'll see. For tonight maybe. But you're going to have to go back sometime. People are worried about you."

I let him stop there. I'm well wet an' shattered, so a bath is enough for now. He clatters around in the kitchen dump he's got an' makes some noise about some dry clothes. Like I'm gonna wear some of Charon's old clothes, yeah *right.* But it's nice that he cares. Can't remember the last time anyone cared this much. After a good long soak, until all my finger are well wrinkled, I gets out, puts this old towel thing on and see that he meant it, he's only gone an' left some baggy old tracksuit type stuff by the door, I'm like,"Mmm, nice."

He goes, "It's not high fashion but it's something warm and dry." I want to kiss him for trying, I really do, even if he says some really stupid things. I goes into the kitchen and I'm like, "Look, Charon, thanks for putting me up. I just need some rest, some food, a chance to get my head together, then I'm gone, I promise. I won't be a burden to you."

"You can stay,"

"No. But I gotta trust you. Tell no-one I'm here. Not even after I'm gone."

"OK. Promise."

"I trust you."

"You can."

"You don't understand. I trust no-one, usually. But I need you. I need someone to trust. It's tiring not having anyone to trust, it's doing my head in. I'm tired of running and I'm tired of not trusting. You gotta promise."

I wanna cry my eyes out after this; I ain't spoken that much to no-one since Ed died. Does Charon mean that much to me? Or am I just desperate? One thing I know; I'm so tired, I'm confused. But I'm also moved to tears. I could kiss him.

167

The Mountain

"I promise." He sounds like he means it.

"If I get caught, they'll stick me in another home, a worse one. I'll never see Darren again, or Dad. You'll get sacked. Can you see how important this is?"

"Yes. You can trust me. I promise."

I well can't cope with this; the emotion is too much. I'm so tired not trustin', an' I want to trust. I think I love him. And then I goes and does it. I lean over, and kiss him on the forehead. Why? I'm so embarrassed now. But I feel really moved.

We sit. We don't chat any longer. He makes some skanky soup from a tin which I can just about eat, actually it's good 'cos it's well hot. We don't talk no more. In any case I'm so tired I could sleep for a thousand years. I quite like the silence and the room is peaceful.

I goes, "Can I sleep somewhere?"

"You must be tired. Take my bed."

"You sure?"

"Sure. I'm quite used to the sofa, anyway."

"Thanks. I'm grateful. I trust you."

I'm gone.

I drift off in his strange room; I've been in that many strange places these last few weeks, I'll wake up tomorrow an' not know where I am. CDs of Bob Dylan and Neil Young are on his bedside table, along with a mass bottle of gin. At one time I'd have taken a swig, listened to the music, too, but I'm dead and listless now.

I drifts off, I've never ever been so tired, but I feel at peace. Johnny Marr's guitar is grinding round my head, I've done no glue or booze but I feel light-headed and at peace. I'm driftin' off and Ed walks into my dream, into this strange bed, and I'm like, "Ed, what you doin'?" when I hears a bell ring really loud and it's not Ed at all, where am I? Oh yeh, Charon's place, only he's got a visitor and that guitar is still grindin' round my head. I hear voices, I hear shoutin', an' I don't know what's goin' on and I feel a bit scared. Why shouldn't Charon have a woman? But I

168

don't like what I hear. I don't like the vibe I get at all. He was so calm, before, almost serene, and I felt we was at peace with each other. Why can't I be at peace? Why do other people's problems and arguments have to mess me up so much?

I look out of the window and the sky is well black. I don't know what the future holds now; I feel all insecure all of a sudden, and scared. I think I've felt this way before. Again and again and again. And it doesn't make me smile.

Chapter 17

"Remove," begins Geoff, "the front wheels after ensuring the jack is firmly in place. Trace the pad wear sensor wiring back from the pad and disconnect it at the wiring connector. Who writes these things?"

A runaway girl is still in my flat and I was threatened four days ago by a mad woman, who has avoided me ever since and, for all I know, is biding her time to wreak some awful revenge. Small talk has never been my forte at the best of times, and Geoff's question must go unanswered.

"Withdraw the pad," continues Geoff, "retaining the split pins and the pads from the calliper. Remove the four pads. The manual's actually from another car but the Daihatsu is similar. Both circuits must be in unison, whatever that means. If there is a hydraulic failure in one, it affects the braking force in two wheels. These have disc brakes as standard."

"Geoff, you may as well be speaking a foreign language. I wouldn't know if you were making it up as you go along. What the hell's a hydraulic failure?"

"You arty farty ponces, no practical skills. Bet you couldn't even change a wheel!"

"I could. I frequently do."

"On a Mini!" Geoff scoffs witheringly. "You wouldn't have a clue on one of these beasts. Go on then! Remove the other front one."

As challenges go this is hardly the stuff to render me indignant, but partly to humour Geoff and partly because there's nothing else to do, I kneel and put the wrench in place. I try to force it down, I even jump on it with all my weight. Nothing moves. Geoff looks pleased.

"I did say these were a different proposition," he presses home his advantage smugly. My clumsy fingers are cold and wet and plainly not up to the job. He takes the wrench and within a minute has undone the wheel.

"Watch and you might learn something. You never know when you might need it. It's all quite complicated behind the wheels of these things, but if you do things methodically and in the right order, you can't go too far wrong, even you. You can help if you want to. Sooner we're finished, sooner we're down the pub. The old bag won't be here to pick it up until after 2."

The job barely takes Geoff half an hour, and we head for his local, The Royal Oak. A few drinks before a single man's Sunday lunch may in part provide me with some comfort. It is a kitschy, tacky pub with cheap worn furnishings in the lounge, but there are worse places to be. Geoff is still in a chatty mood.

"So, how'd'you find school after half a term or so? Think you'll stay? They aren't such a bad bunch!"

"There must be worse places. I'll cope."

"How's the old discipline coming on? Any easier?"

"Last week a kid told me to fuck off and ran off. Told both Marshall and Gillespie he wasn't speaking to me."

"My God, what they do nowadays! Still, there are many worse places than Chapelton. It's just that, well, many of these kids don't have any hope."

I'd rather talk about brake pads and retaining pins than this, but Geoff is on a roll.

"You see, the heart was taken out of this community and never replaced. When they shut the last pits they put the final nail in the coffin of these people.

The Mountain

Now they have nothing to aim for, no hope, no future, no jobs. They're the salt of the earth, but-"

"For God's sake Geoff, how many clichés can you pack into one sentence? And they're not all the salt of the earth. Pooch in my German class isn't the salt of the sodding earth. Neither's Yacker Smith."

Not for the first time I have been sharp and unfair towards Geoff. He falls silent, chastened, and the irony that I sympathise with most of his somewhat simplistic analysis hits me, as usual, too late. I try to make amends:

"Pint?"

"What? Yeah go on. Got ages 'till that old witch gets here."

"Does she pay you?"

"What, in cashew and lentil roasts? In Laura Ashley tokens? No way. She's out for what she can get for herself, and doesn't mind who she uses."

I am surprised by the sudden reversal in our roles. Geoff now dons the mantle of world weary cynic, while I resort to the small talk I usually eschew.

"So…she's not your favourite person at the moment?"

Geoff mellows a little.

"Oh, she's not that bad. She has a bad life. Husband's a prat. It's just that when she and Eleanor are together I find them kind of hard work. So false and, well, not entirely trustworthy, I think."

"How d'you mean?"

"Not sure. It's just that, well, I feel she'd stab you in the back as soon as look at you, especially if there was something in it for her."

These words do nothing to ease my mind, so I decide to suspend the small talk and we both pretend to watch a football match on the TV in the far corner of the room. Then, with what could be the timing of a particularly malevolent theatre director, the door opens suddenly and Judy breezes in.

172

The Mountain

"Hi boys, thought I might find you in here."

"Judy," Geoff splutters. "Didn't expect you so soon. We've only just got here."

"But youse'll have time for another, I hope?"

"Yes. Car's done. Nigel even helped a bit."

"A man of hidden talents."

Judy has not looked at me since entering the room and both talk about me as if I had in fact left. When our drinks arrive the dialogue continues.

"Take you long?" asks Judy.

"No, half an hour or so. They were well worn, mind."

"Oh well I'm very grateful."

"What friends are for."

"And what does this afternoon hold?"

"Few jobs to do on my car, actually. Bodywork's got more holes in it that an old pair of tights. In fact, I-"

Judy drains her glass of wine.

"But first, you'll have another?"

"Christ, hold on! Only just got this! You're in a rush!"

"I'm a thirsty girl! And it *is* Sunday." She turns to me for the first time. "Nigel, you ready for another? Go on!"

In fact I have been drinking as quickly as possible in order to be able to leave as soon as possible, but it is now too late; the dreaded drink appears. To make matters worse, Geoff is now making good progress with his, although not good enough to justify a refill. Thus we will remain out of phase with each other, and we are both well aware that the first one apart from Judy with an empty glass will leave the pub as soon as is respectably possible. Suddenly I hate Geoff, if only for the pace of his drinking.

One o' clock chimes on the tacky mantelpiece clock and right on cue Geoff drains his glass, says "Aaaah!" and stands up in the manner of a husband of some fifty years standing who knows that his roast beef and

173

The Mountain

Yorkshires have now been on the table for just as long as is acceptable. And when he says: "Gotta go, now. Places to go, people to see, I'll love you and leave you." I really do want to hit him.

Now it is Judy's time to drain her glass, again.

"Well, is my other knight in shining armour ready for another?"

"What?" I try to put a lot of indignation into the word.

"Well, you helped with my car," she explains sunnily. "I'd be stuck without you boys. Pity Geoff couldn't stay…"

"Well, can I get you one?"

"Thought you'd never ask. A large red wine please. Cabernet Sauvignon. And you may like another."

My glass is still half empty and I am uneasy about her apparent concern for my thirst.

"I have something I need to show you."

I order a half for myself and the red wine. There is something very disquieting about Judy's manner and I sit down and stare at my shoes. She takes a long and painstakingly slow sip of her wine before saying:

"That's *not* Cabernet Sauvignon. Or if it is,"-and she somehow manages to make this sound like a far worse crime-"then it's either Bulgarian or Romanian."

"It's the end of the world. Now what did you want to show me? I have things to do myself this afternoon."

"Oh, I'm quite sure you have. Maybe they can wait. I hope they can wait. D'you think we can get a bite to eat in this place?"

"Oh I'm sure the barman will rustle you up a Sushi sandwich."

"In here? I *doubt* it."

"What did you want to show me?"

"Oh, *that*!" she replies with studied indifference. "Well, just…this," and produces a crumpled piece of paper.

174

The Mountain

"A piece of paper."

"Not just *any* piece," she says with relish. This must be how she gets her kicks. "Let's see now…I don't recognise the handwriting. The gist of it is…well, I'll quote from the source, shall I?"

"Please do."

"Since you insist. It's addressed to Charon. 'If you ever cared anything about me, meet me again in the park, at 6, on Wednesday.' Sounds good. Wonder who it's from. I've been mulling it over inside my head, time and time again. And then something clicked. That was last Wednesday. When I came round to yours. No wonder you wanted rid of me."

"Judy-"

"Then there's this bit. 'Whatever you do don't tell anyone.' That intrigued me, still does. You're seeing someone else, I can live with that. But it's obviously someone you shouldn't be seeing. Yet another married woman? But then I thought, why meet in the park? You'd surely meet another woman in a pub off the beaten track, or in a car. So guess what I think?"

I feel sick and I see stars in front of my eyes. My mouth is dry and my fingers tremble. And then I wonder: can she see the sweat on my face and neck? Can she smell the fear?

"I think, and I think you know that I think, that it's a kid at school. It's a pupil!! I'm right, aren't I? Personable, handsome young man like you flatters a young girl's vanity. It can happen. It gets better. 'I need you desperately.' Why would that be, Nigel? What's so desperate about this girl and her need? She sounds like she's in some kind of trouble. Who is this 'A'?"

I pretend not to know what she is talking about, but there is little point and even less chance of success. But I will go down fighting.

"Where did you get that?"

The Mountain

"That's for me to know, Nigel. Have I hit a little nerve?"

"That could have been found anywhere, been written by anyone? You're surely not going to take it seriously. It'll be a hoax. Kids write prank notes like that all the time."

"Nice try, Nigel. Any idea where I found this note?"

I am at this stage so attuned to dissembling mode that being honest rather disorientates me. But I think for a minute, honestly, and answer in the same way:

"No."

"Your flat."

"What?"

"When you turned me down, when you kicked me out, I swept up my handbag and keys from your kitchen table, and stomped off in super-quick time. I must have swept up the incriminating note, too, amongst some tissues and God knows whatever else you had on your filthy table-top. Didn't notice it until I got home that evening, but I've been meaning to discuss it with you."

I am stunned. I remember now emptying the contents of my sodden pockets onto the kitchen table before getting changed. The table-top was such a mess that Judy took half of its contents with her belongings. In one sense this situation arose because of the squalor of my flat, and in another, paradoxically, it was my instinct to get tidied up which made me the author of what looks like being my downfall.

"Can you explain?" probes Judy gently.

"What do you plan to do?"

"And what would you do, if you were me?"

"It's not what it looks like…"

"What is it then, Nigel?"

"It's… I…it's delicate. Someone's in a spot of trouble. Oh, OK then, it's that troubled Anna in my form. I'm sworn to secrecy. I'd appreciate it if you didn't…"

The Mountain

Judy is suddenly the hard-nosed inquisitor.

"You listen to me. I don't believe you for one minute, so don't even begin to think that I do. The first time you refused me I said that you didn't want to make an enemy of me. Then last Wednesday I told you that you didn't want to cross me. How thick are you, Nigel? And do you think for one moment that you're in a position to turn me down a third time?"

"What?"

"It's so simple, Nigel. It's beautiful in its simplicity. From now on, you do what I want, when I want it. Beginning to understand me?"

I swallow more loudly that I mean to.

"And for your information, Nigel," she announces loudly, "I want it now."

Chapter 18

The first time I did E was last summer, the so-called second summer of love, some joke. It was about the only day that whole long sodding wet summer when I nearly felt happy. I felt relaxed, almost like my muscles had stopped doin' anythin' for themselves, I felt good for an hour an' me an' Becky an' Tracey went out to this warehouse near Manchester with some of their other mates. I felt good on the way there, I felt good there too, listenin' to the Happy Mondays an' the Charlatans, not really my music (Smiths fans don't do E, too poncey, they're more into cider an' glue) but good music all the same an' a good rave, and on the train on the way back I felt warm an' comfortable, in fact warmer than I had for a good while before or since. The skanky train seats were like huge cushions to me, cushions on a big four-poster bed. Seven months since Eddie dies, an' that was the first day I felt anything like alright, an' one of the last times. The E helped forget all the bad, evil things in the world that were happenin', Eddie dead, Mum gone, Dad's empty sunken eyes without any feeling, without any hope. £25 we had to nick, from Becky an' Tracey's, but it felt good, an' I've always gone back to it when we've been in the money.

So now, holed up at Charon's, I feel a bit mellow an' I feel a bit safe, like it's gonna be OK. An' I've held on to this half a tab for almost a month now, an' now's a good time to drop it, he's out the house an' the Mondays are playin' around my head as I lie in his bath again.

178

The Mountain

together, it's better than hostels or school, and Charon
cares, I think he cares.

So I goes into the kitchen, where he's got sod all,
to make anything out of any of this mess is gonna be a right

The Mountain

We ain't spoken much. On Wednesday I just
crashed out after the bath, slept most of Thursday. Tried to
tidy up his hovel of a flat on Thursday, an' today I'm just
enjoyin' havin' the place to myself, although I like when he
comes back, too, it gives be a warm, safe feeling. I'm
nervous that someone'll knock on the door, although the E
has calmed my nerves now an' I'm mellowed out. In a
strange way, though, I kind of like watching the clock and
waiting for someone to come home. It's kind of nice, and
then I think, yeah, when was the last time you looked
forward to someone coming home? When was the last
time you looked forward to anything?

I don't really do self-pity, no point, so these
thoughts don't take up too much space in my head,
'specially as there's other things crammin' it, like: what
happens next week? Where do I go? What happens to
Darren? What will he say when he sees me? Does he
think I've left him for good? What will happen to Charon?
What will happen to Charon an'me? Where's Dad?
Where's Mum?

An' then I think, you stupid selfish cow, you
wrecked everything, why couldn't you have just stayed
put? That place weren't so bad, an' now they'll probably
put me some place worse, away from Darren. And what's
been goin' through his mind, abandoned yet again? Does
he really believe I went off lookin' for Dad? Do I believe
it myself? An' it's not as important, but I realise I've made
things difficult for Charon, too. Who knows whether he
really wanted to get involved with me? Why should he?
Well he's involved now, and what will his mates say, if he
has mates? What if they find out?

I do do anxiety, I do it big time. Plenty of
practice, plenty of reason to do it. You don't look after a
family for a short time, even a crappy one like ours,
without doin' loads of anxiety. But then I think, hey, why
wreck the last day, or one of the last days of freedom? So I
try to enjoy bein' here alone, waitin' for Charon.

179

The Mountain
"Thanks for making some food.   That was
thoughtful of you." But there should be more to it than
this.

        Saturday is no better. I'm holed up in his dump of
a flat, he's out with his mates, drinkin' or watchin' football
or talkin' about cars or whatever it is that mates do. His
phone keeps ringin' so there must be one mate he hasn't
caught up with. Then early afternoon someone knocks on
the door, I jumps out of my skin! What if it's the pigs?
Osborne? What if whoever it is has a key? I'm brickin' it
an' can't keep silent enough, I keep twitching and his
manky old floorboards are creakin'. And then I hear it – a
woman's voice. "Nigel? Coo-ee? Nigel? Are you in
there, Nigel? If so, come out. We need to talk." I've
heard this sort of stuff in films an' that, but this time it's
real. Except do real people really say coo-ee? My body is
too big behind this kitchen door, she's gonna see my
shadow, she's gonna hear my heart beatin' crazily. She
stays for ten minutes except it feels like ten hours. Well at
least she ain't the pigs.
        Charon don't get back till about 6, at least he's
less wasted than last night. When I tell him he goes white.
        "Anna, we've got to get you out of here. No-one
can find you here."
        I'm like, "but tonight's our last night. It was
gonna be special." This sounds crap, at least I haven't
cremated any food for him this time, but I still wanted a
nice evening together. I'm like, "Where can I go? The
caravan? Osborne's? Youth club? School? Pigs'll be all
over town lookin' for me."
        Charon agrees, but has this plan that I don't like.
We have to turn all the lights out an' pretend no-one's in.
So no food, not even burnt food, no music, not even his 70s
stuff, certainly no candlelit atmosphere. Then about 9 he'll
sneak out and see his waster mates in a pub just for a

182

out on the tops for ages. I'm growin' stale in here an'
suddenly this crappy little flat smells of old man, an' I
don't like it no more. But then I have to pull myself

change, they'll be so far gone by the end of the evening that no-one'll remember he hadn't been there all evening, or at least most of it. A perfect alibi. An' me? I'll spend our last evening together in the cold, brickin' it, waitin' for the 'phone or doorbell to ring. Oh an' I'll be on my own. Nice evening together? Nice evenings don't happen to scumbags like me.

Chapter 19

I return with two drinks.

"Judy, don't be hasty."

"Charon, you're not in a position to tell anyone what to do and what not to do." The use of my surname from her is unfamiliar and reminds me of how very much she is in the driving seat. At this precise moment in walk Eleanor and David; I don't know whether to laugh or cry.

"Eleanor!" I do quite a good job of sounding quite pleased. "How are you?" It was the wrong question to ask. "I'm…OK…" she ventures. This is delivered in the tone of voice which could reasonably be expected from, say, a blind-folded tightrope walker crossing Niagara Falls on being asked about his progress. Pausing to kiss her friend on both cheeks, Eleanor heroically makes it as far as the table and manages to sit down.

"I think," thunders David unnecessarily, "our friend Eleanor may be a little under the weather. I met her outside and suggested we come in for a little pick-me-up. Not…interrupting anything, are we?"

"No, no, we're gid, gid" is Judy's version of thinking on her feet.

"Actually I was just going," is my version, scarcely an improvement.

"Stuff and nonsense! Stay," counters David, "and cheer up poor ailing Lady Eleanor. You look about ready for another one." I don't want to be here, but I could be in a worse place. So I stay.

The Mountain

"Have you told them about next Saturday, babe?" asks the poor ailing lady of her friend. For someone so close to death's door a minute ago she has perked up remarkably.

"No, I was going to wait 'till we were all together?" Judy's mood, too seems to have improved, although that was the only possible change of direction for it. "But since you asked so sweetly…Ok, um, don't tell everyone, but, next Saturday we're having a bit of a do over at Brown Hill. Frances' Mason buddies – oh, they're a ghastly crew, a motley mob or whatever the expression, is, but there's always a good spread. We get caterers in from Sheffield."

"Not the organic deli?" asks Eleanor, although I am sure she knows the answer.

"Darling, but of course. Frances doesn't know whether to go Thai or Greek. What he knows about fid…he simply wants an excuse to throw his money about. Anyway, the victuals will look after themselves, his wine club delivery from last week should see us in libation. *Do* say you'll both join us."

"As two", responds David, "of the great imbibers of the age, we will be glad to join you, won't we, Charon?"

"Actually," I begin weakly and promptly disintegrate.

"Come now, Hades' ferryman! What can you be doing that's so important? Transporting dead souls across the river Styx?"

His remark is greeted by blank looks, following which Judy warms to her theme. "Shall we say 4 for 4.30? It's a beastly road when it's dark, best to arrive a little before. You can all stay over. I have to drive down the hill the next morning to catch the man with the quails' eggs from the market. Frances can rustle us all up an omelette, if he's not too useless to do that. Hopefully his boring cronies will have long since gone."

"Oh, my God, I love omelettes made with quails' eggs," is Eleanor's contribution. "Simply to die for!"

185

The Mountain

Quite abruptly Judy drains her glass. "Well, Nigel",
she begins, "if you're going to show me those French
poems you're always banging on about, perhaps we should
make tracks. Symbolists probably make marginally more
sense before it gets too dark, or before one's judgement is
too clouded by too much of this plonk. Not that that ever
seemed to stop *them.* And I'd better get back to him
indoors before nightfall, too." She stops short of actually
kicking me under the table, but there is no mistaking my
cue to go.

The walk from The Royal Oak to my flat takes
about twenty minutes and, surprisingly for two people who
should have quite a bit to say to each other, we spend it in
silence. It is only as we approach the building that I slow
down my pace and take a deep breath.

"There's something you need to know," I tell her.

"Go on, lover boy." Is she being playful or hostile? I
hesitate.

"The girl is in my flat."

"Oh, this just gets better," she screams. "Warming
your bed, is she? Well, I'm sure she'll be overjoyed to see
someone from school, especially her favourite deputy-head
of year. We can catch up on some gossip."

"You can't come in."

"Nigel, maybe I haven't made myself clear. The thing
about me and ultimatums-"

"I mean it, you can't come in." Now my voice is
raised. She'll freak. She'll do a runner. She's unstable."

"Nigel, do I have to remind you that you're not in a
position to tell me what to do?"

"She'll do a runner. She'll get caught, taken back
into care. She'll be split up from her brother. It'll destroy
her! She'll never trust another adult again."

Judy gives me a very withering look. "You should
have thought of that before you invited her into your bed."

186

And with that, she grabs the keys from my hand and turns the front door lock.

I pray for the impossible – that Anna has left the flat, or, equally improbably, that Judy can't find her in it – but it is in vain. Anna is standing in the middle of my wretched kitchen which the front door opens directly onto and looks completely exposed. Judy's face bears a look of malicious satisfaction.

"Well, well, well!" begins Judy, with all the heavy sarcasm of one who has mastered her trade. She brandishes Anna's ill-advised note in Pyrrhic triumph. "Whom do we have here? If it isn't our very own little feral runaway! So my informants in that Art cover lesson weren't so wrong! Shacking up with your teacher! It's…pathetic! Distasteful! And most probably illegal. Nigel, leave us!"

"Actually," I falter, "I think you'll find this is-

"Nigel!!"
"I think-"
"Out!!"
"But-"
"Now!!"

This is an argument I am losing, but before I have the chance to obey her, she returns her attention to Anna.

"Now then, you little slag! There's attention seeking and there's attention seeking. Sleeping with your teacher! How desperate can you get? He doesn't even like you! He doesn't give a shit about you and your kind! You're *nothing*-"

At this Anna lets out an animal-like, blood-curdling shriek, quite the loudest I have ever heard, picks up a plate from the kitchen table, hurls it frisbee-style at Judy, barely missing her but smashing into large sharp pieces as it hits the wall. She then makes to grab one of the pieces and lunge at Judy with it, changes her mind and bolts out of the still open front door.

187

The Mountain

"Crazy, sick, demented bitch!" shouts Judy, either at her or about her. "She could have killed me!"

"Judy, I'm so sorry!" I reply weakly, not for the first time this afternoon. "Are you OK?"

"Am I OK? Am I OK? The man I am seeing is cheating on me with a pupil, a crazed bitch who tries to kill me, and you find time to wonder if I'm OK?"

"Technically I'm not actually-"

"Technically?! Technically?! Do you think this is any time for your bloody technically?" As if to underline her words, she picks a large shard of plate from the floor and hurls it at my face. Her aim is better than Anna's and a serious dodge on my part is required to avoid it. The fragment of plate continues its trajectory toward the small kitchen window which it smashes.

Judy then collapses onto a kitchen chair and puts her head in her hands. I have the impression the reprieve is quite temporary and hesitate. This does not seem the time to offer a cup of tea, Lapsang -Souchong or otherwise. I decide no action is the wisest course.

I sit and rummage around my thoughts. Why have I made things so difficult for myself? Why Anna? Why have her here? Why ever get involved with Judy at all? This last couple of weeks have been up and down and all over the place. If that's possible simultaneously. I've thought I've been caught, then thought I've been in the clear, then flirted with danger again, then thought I've been safe…Every time I've felt safe, I've complicated things and made matters worse for myself. I've given myself several mountains to climb. On this last occasion it was simply too much to ask for.

About fifteen minutes later Judy revives herself, uses my bathroom noisily for a short while, and returns in brisk, matter-of-fact mode, picking up random objects from the floor and harassing her handbag fastener. Then she sits down again. She says:

188

The Mountain

"Lick Charon, I will be civil with you. For appearances' sake. I don't need to be embroiled in a scandal – it sometimes seems to be that that is what you are trying to do to yourself, for whatever reason, but that's your problem. I don't need it. You and I are completely finished. I seem to remember at one stage you said something like 'there is no us'. Well, just for once you were right, you snotty little pedant. There *is* no us.

I won't say anything to our colleagues, as far as they are concerned, things are as normal, whatever the hell that means. Christ knows what it means in your world. But as far as they can see, we'll carry on as normal. You'll keep going to the pub to get wrecked with your tiresome friends, Eleanor and I will occasionally drop in for you to make fun of us, then go off on our rounds. I couldn't bear anyone knowing what has just happened here.

You might as well know this, too. I wasn't quite right when I said 'no-one' just then – I'll save you the bother of having to pick me up on that. I'm reporting that little bitch to the police. Attempted assault. That will be the least of her problems when they find her. Which they will. By tonight. Expect a visit from them. Harbouring a runaway minor. And that, chum, is the very least of *your* problems. You should go into school tomorrow as usual, at a guess, and go straight to old man White's office. You'll be suspended pending the enquiry, that's the term. But make no mistake about it, Charon, you're finished at Chapelton High." She pauses. "To be honest, you never even started."

She looks crest-fallen, ashen-faced, upset beyond words and yet somehow serene as she makes for the open door. She turns to me and says: "One thing Charon. Was she worth it? Really?"

Chapter 20

A dreaded Sunday. An' I'm gonna try and be positive. I've always hated them. Grim and grey. Like a forgotten seaside town. Well this Sunday's gonna be different. For one thing, it's almost sunny outside. It's my last day here. Me an' Charon knew it couldn't last. So rather than be caught, I'll hand myself in. What's the worst that can happen? I'll hand myself in an' go back to Osborne's poxy home. I never thought I'd say it, but I might have to play by their rules. Just for a bit. They may even let me see Darren. We may even find out about Dad. I said I were bein' positive.

I'm not tellin' them where I've been though. Why should I? School can't force me. I'm probably done with school anyway. Pigs can't make me. Osborne'll be too busy bakin' me a cake or summat. It wouldn't do for him to be heavy-handed or owt. An' that way Charon's in the clear. No-one need know I've been here. Anyway he's done nowt wrong. But I guess he don't need the scandal. All he done were tryin' to look out for me, like no-one else done. But people who try to look out for others get nowt in return but grief. I know that from Darren.

Anyway, in the morning Charon says he's gotta go to the pub just for a change, only this time to 'keep up appearances'. He actually says that! I didn't think he cared about crap like appearances, no offence like. But he explains that everything has to be as normal in the eyes of others, or summat. So if that means goin' to some dump of

190

The Mountain

a pub an' getting' wrecked with his arsehole mates, that's what he's gotta do.

So it's our last day an' I'm left alone. But I understand it's best. I sits an' mopes around the house. Watch his soddin' clock tickin' in slow motion. Where's Darren? Where's Dad? Where's Becky an' Tracey? Why can't I just go back to how things were, have a laugh with them, skank some fags an' glue from the shop, get some old git to buy some cider for us? I just want things to be like they were again. They weren't great, but just for a minute, I want them like they were anyway. Uncomplicated. I'm tired of runnin' an' hidin'. I'm cold.

All I know is: Mum loved me, once. Ed loved me. Charon's tried to look out for me. An' I'm cold. Charon's been gone a couple of hours. It's sunny outside. I dread sunny days. I don't do sunny. It's not what I do. I'm black on the outside an' inside, an' I'm cold.

An' then, just as it's beginning to get dark, I think a crazy thought – I wanna go for a run. I need to go for a run. I've been holed up in this crap flat for days, I need to run in the hills. But it's crazy, it's crazier than crazy. If someone sees me, if I'm caught, it'll make everything bad, everything'll be ruined. Charon'll be found out for hiding me, pigs'll be heavy with me an' give me a hard time, even Granny Osborne'll not be too pleased to see me. If I go out, I'll get caught.

But I need to. It's like a drug – I don't even mean the runnin', it's the risk that's like the drug, it's like I can't cope with bein' safe an' I wanna make things worse for myself. So I gets on my black T shirt an' leggins an' climbs out of Charon's back bedroom window.

It backs onto Grindey Woods. By this time poncey snotty Volvo-drivin' snobs will be walkin' back down through the woods with Francesca an' Jeremy an' the scuffin' labrador an' headin' for home, the posh part of

191

The Mountain

Park Road or Cavendish Lane, where the grandfather clock
will be chimin' an' the smell of Sunday roast will be
beginnin' to waft through the downstairs reception room
into the study. I pulls a woollen hat over my face an'
begins to run, head down at all times.

It feels good – I've missed it. Blood rushes to my head
as I breathe in the cold dry air. Rain would feel better, but
it's OK. Up the muddy path, past the ash an' beech trees,
avoiding happy families on the way back to civilisation.
Pigs'd be too thick to look here. They like their routine,
an' they'll be like – caravan, youth centre, school *(why?)*,
shops, offies, Tracey's, Becky's, Osborne's home *(why?)*,
although if anyone cared enough to find out what I do
they'd know I run, they'll be too thick an' too lazy to come
up here.

I run all the way up to the cross at the top, quick as I
can so's not to be seen, I feel faint, well it's been a long
time, but I also feel good. Although I don't like the sun I
like the cold, it feels good on my face. An' I want to stop
for a while up here, just to look round, but I know I can't.
People are here (people are my enemy) an' just supposin'
Charon ever gets back from his social engagements he'd
freak if he saw I was gone. It's gettin' dark, which is
good.

By the time I'm back at Charon's it's nearly
completely dark, which is also good. It makes climbin'
back in his bedroom window without bein' seen easy. An'
for the first time in ages, I feel really good. I'm glad I
went. I'm glad I'm gonna be with Charon soon. An' in a
weird way, I'm glad I'm quittin' hidin' tonight. I have a
quick shower, then another weird thought hits me. I'm
gonna make myself look nice for Charon. Our last evening
together. Nothin' over the top, a clean black T shirt, my
long black skirt that I like. An' I'm gettin' out the shower

192

an' I'm even thinkin' about puttin' on some Goth make-up, big panda eyes like Robert Smith.

My mood is almost good, an' I'm listenin' to The Cure, *Lovesong* from *Disintegration*, as I'm puttin' on make-up for the first time I can remember. An' then suddenly there's a hell of a commotion outside, a full Lloyd Cole, an' there's shoutin' an' screamin, an' I hears Charon's voice, an' there's a woman's voice I think I recognise. An' the door opens.

I don't believe it. It's only that cow Hartington. Of all people. She goes, "Well, well, well," in that sarky teacher tone they all use with me. "And who do we have here?" all that kind of stuff. An' I'm all pathetic an' all the rest, apparently. Then the words just bounce off the walls an' fly over my head an' I don't hear them no more.

I don't hear them 'cos I can't take it all in. What is Charon doing with her? Why has he brought her back here? Is she just a mate from the pub? Is he seeing her? Even so, why the hell would he bring her back here, knowin' that I'm here? It don't make sense. Except, obviously, he don't give a stuff about me. He never has. She's wavin' a piece of paper in the air, then she's yellin' at Charon, then at me. Callin' me a slag, attention seekin', desperate. The worst thing she says is that he don't give a shit about me.

An' the worst thing about that is, it's probably true.

So I goes mental an' I chuck this skanky plate at her ugly bitch's face, miss her, pity, but the plate hits the wall. I tries to grab a bit of plate an' stab her scrawny neck with it, I don't care what happens to me after this. All this time Charon doesn't have the guts to say a single word, he just stands there like he's scared of her. I can't stand the idea of him carin' so little he don't, he won't even say owt. I'm lookin, across at him, beggin' him with my big panda eyes. Nowt.

So much for me bein' positive. So much for me feelin' good today. So much for our last evening together. Ever.

193

The Mountain

What I really can't stand is how much I trusted him. With bastards like Gillespie, you know where you stand. You know they scuffin' hate you an' your kind. You know where you are with the pigs, too. An' it's not good, but it's better like that. At least you don't feel so let down.

An' I'm out of here, double quick. Dunno where, but I'm gone. I rush out the door, tear off my black skirt an' in just my T shirt an' black leggings I run an' run.

Chapter 21

The next morning, instead of the usual alarm clock it is the telephone which awakens me. It is 8 am. An emotionless voice at the other end says: "Mr Charon? Chapelton High School here, reception speaking. Please do not come into school until 1.30 pm, when you are requested to go straight to Dr White's office. Do not go to the staffroom or into the main part of the school."

On the radio there is a song playing something about someone not caring if Monday is blue or not, as he is in love on another day. This Monday feels more numb than anything else to me. In a daze I wash and shave, put on my suit and tie to try to look like what they might deem appropriate. I leave the flat and begin my condemned man's walk, my walk of shame.

I did this walk for the first time back in September. Then as now it rained. The streets and houses are still as shabby and grey, the school gates the same mixture of green and rust, even the gang of smoking youths by the leisure centre is still present. In some ways, nothing has changed. I didn't feel I was destined to fit in then, and I certainly don't now.

I look at the tall glass and concrete tower block which houses A block, a kind of Soviet-style apartment building which somehow I overlooked on that first day. Who designs these places? The Victorians, with all their flaws and separate boys' and girls' entrances, at least

195

The Mountain

designed schools with some feeling, with curves. This shambles is all straight lines and brutal right angles, an essai in rigidity, in heartlessness. And hopelessness. How to inspire a generation of children.

Thus stimulated I wait outside Dr White's office, where a traffic light system announces his availability. It is on bright red: engaged. The receptionist occasionally looks up from her typewriter to examine her nails. It is 1.30.

Ten minutes later there is a flurry of activity as one, two, then three be-suited and important looking gentlemen exit the office. The light changes to amber: wait.

Upon its becoming green (please knock) I summon up courage and approach the door. As beckoned, I knock.

"Come!" chimes a thin, bloodless voice.

I enter the room, in which Dr White in his full graduate's gown is seated at the head of an imposing oak table, flanked by five other be-suited gentlemen, Anthony Marshall, John Gillespie, and Judy Hartington. I can hear the blood thumping inside my temples.

"Mr Charon," he begins. He doesn't actually say welcome, as he did back in September, but the tone of voice is identical. "In accordance with the Teachers' Disciplinary Regulations, we have convened at short notice a professional conduct panel. May I introduce to you: Mr Evans and Mr Ronson from the LEA, Mr Gibson the Chair of Governors, Mr Lewis and Mr Mathews, also from the governing body." He leers as he cranes forward. "Ms Hartington, Mr Marshall and Mr Gillespie, you…" he pauses, "already know."

I am invited to give my account of events. Judy Hartington gives hers. They differ. I am invited to wait outside while the panel deliberates. They do not seem to take long.

"Mr Charon," beckons a familiar reedy voice. "Do please…enter."

The Chair of Governors speaks.

196

The Mountain

"Mr Charon, um, this would appear to be a complex case. We have heard two, um, differing accounts of your conduct, and it is not within the remit of this panel to reach a firm decision this morning. We will examine all the evidence, with, um, witness statements. These are serious allegations, Mr Charon - abuse of position involving vulnerable pupils, serious departure from the personal and professional conduct elements of the teachers' professional code of conduct, and possibly serious sexual misconduct. We will reconvene at a later date but you must be warned that there is a possibility of the, um, panel recommending a prohibition order to the Secretary of State. Until that time, you are suspended from duty on full pay. This is a neutral act and should not be seen as a pre-judgment of the issues, nor does it imply any guilt or, um, wilful misconduct on your part. During this period it is strongly recommended that you do not enter the school premises or make contact with any pupils or employees."

Without signalling anything to each other in any visible form, the five suits then stand up as one, rearrange the pens in their outside breast pockets, fidget with their Filofaxes, then bid Dr White good-day and leave. I didn't particularly like them being here, but now that they are gone I feel somehow more exposed.

There is what feels like a long silence, which Dr White breaks with these words:

"Mr Charon, Mr Charon, Mr Char*on*!" with what I feel is undue emphasis on the last syllable. Quite how I am to respond to this eludes me, but he carries on.

"*Mr* Charon! What an untidy mess! What a lamentable situation! What a tangled web!" It is difficult to tell because of the oak table, but I sense that Gillespie and Marshall are trying to look at their feet – I know I am. Judy Hartington looks no-where in particular.

"Mr Charon," he continues. "You must leave the building at the soonest possible opportunity. Do not go to the staffroom to collect your things. They can be…*dealt*

197

with at some other stage. And Mr Charon," he pauses, from my point of view possibly for the last time, "whatever the outcome of this sorry tale, you might use your leave of absence to ponder some, shall we say, career direction changes?" I look at Judy Hartington. She is smirking.

"And now, gentlemen," he concludes, "I have an important meeting with Mr Evans and the 5th year pastoral team, as you can perhaps imagine. We will leave Mr Charon in your capable hands, Mr Marshall." And three-fifths of the room empties.

The ensuing pause seems unduly long. No accomplished wordsmith, Marshall seems particularly tongue-tied, as he eventually stutters:

"Well, young Nigel! What a to-do! You may – actually I think the old man's advice is sound. You weren't really cut out for here. Can't say I blame you, either. Bright young chap like you, you'll get another job somewhere. You'll bounce back! Now I don't want to pry," he leans forward so I can smell his sweaty armpits more, "but, well, correct me if I'm wrong, no, I don't want to pry, but, well, is there a little bit of a whiff of 'Hell hath no fury' about this? Hmm?"

"Can't think what you might mean, Anthony," I reply sourly. "And anyway, I'm supposed to avoid talking to my ex-colleagues."

"Oh come on, I saw the look on Judy's face. And I saw that you saw it, too."

He's fat and he's useless, but well-meaning. He of all people does not deserve my vitriol. But he gets it.

"Haven't you got some marking you should be doing?" I say, and I get up and leave the room, probably also for the last time.

That's me then. No job, no mates, come to that no personal contact with anyone. Quite the little 'persona non grata', as Stanton might possibly say. Except not to me. Not any longer, anyway.

The Mountain

I have a lot of time to kill. I wander around these dismal streets until I can take it no longer. I gaze uninterestedly into shop windows. I make a couple of pointless purchases then walk slowly back to my flat. There, the memories of last night, which could have been so happy, are too raw to bear. It's odd that things unravelled as Anna and I were trying to do the right thing. But they were always going to unravel at some stage. Where is Anna now? I'm feeling sorry for myself, but what does her future hold?

I can't stand it in here so leave almost immediately. I walk the streets again. Nowhere to go, no-one to go there with. I think of a drink. It's nearly 4 pm. All-day pub opening has caught on, even in this backwater, so it is a possibility, but I must choose my venue with care. Thus, like a fugitive, I make my way towards the Royal Oak.

If the pub's décor is not inspiring, its choice as a venue was nonetheless inspired. Save for two labourers beating hell out of a fruit machine, it is well and truly empty. I order a pint with a large whisky chaser and sit down in a window seat to read my newspaper. The words – I can see them on the page. But they didn't reach me.

My time in France ended abruptly. Of course I was never going to finish my thesis comparing two anarchist romantics – when had I ever seen anything through? After Gianluca's funeral I became more entrenched in the family, a lover for Marcia to replace Paolo and companion to replace Gianluca. And the extended family were grateful to me. I was the cause of half of their problems, and they were grateful to me.

I decided when and how I was going to leave. It would break Marcia's fragile little heart, but I couldn't bear to stay. That spring, the extended family were having a

The Mountain

*celebratory meal to mark the forthcoming engagement of
her younger brother, Amato. The beloved one.*

*Leaving was risky, but in the end easy. Towards
midnight, after most of the dancing, the old men drained
their grappas, the old women fussed about the food, the
plates, the washing. The young couples continued to dance
sporadically, some chatted and walked hand in hand in the
cool night air, the terrace of the hotel offering respite from
the stifling cauldron that was the interior.*

*It should have been Marcia and me walking arm in
arm on the terrace. But she understood how I felt these
family occasions cloying, she understood me and showed
no reaction when I excused myself from the dance floor.*

*On my way out of the back door I saw Amato smoking
with two friends. And they saw me. And they said nothing
– I knew they never would. And following the course of the
moonlit river towards the town, I ran and I ran.*

Lost in my thoughts, I might have expected the time to
go quickly. It hasn't. I have had four drinks now and it is
barely after 5. And then, what I didn't want to happen does
happen. The door opens and in walks Geoff Lennox. The
only good thing is that he's alone.

"Well," he starts, and continues not unreasonably, "you
look like you've been here for some time. You're the
subject of considerable gossip back at the ranch. Staying
for another?"

"It'll pass the time. But I'm not supposed to talk to
you."

I am very nearly as good as my word. I can't confirm
or deny any of Geoff's rumours, which have some basis in
accuracy but appear to have been filtered through Judy
Hartington. He seems frustrated by my taciturn nature,
then suddenly changes tack.

"Anyway, what about 4 for 4.30?"
"What?"

The Mountain

"You so sozzled you don't remember yesterday? Black Ridge? Next Saturday? Frances? Thai or Greek?"

"Oh, Christ. Actually I had rather put it to the back of my mind. Events got in the way. Had a rather eventful afternoon after we left you."

"Yes, I'd gathered. Why don't you come with me?"

"Oh, I don't know. I'm not supposed to see people from work. If I say anything-"

"Oh, for God's sake! In the presence of *her*, of all people, you're not going to talk about…events. It'll be a laugh! What have you got to lose? Why don't we meet in here about 3, I'll take you there."

I have been in here for too long. Against my better judgment, if such a thing exists, I agree to meeting him on Saturday.

When Saturday comes I feel emboldened by one of the last questions Geoff asked me – what have I got to lose? I am in trouble anyway, it is difficult to see how the situation could be any worse, so I might as well go. What have I got to lose?

The same rationale takes me to one or two of the town's less salubrious drinking dens in the early afternoon, searching for any clues to Anna's whereabouts – her friends, anyone who knows her father, anything. I choose The Red Lion and The White Hart. At my best I am a less than convincing sleuth, but even the meagre skills that I possess evaporate gradually the more liquid I consume as I am meant to be pursuing my enquiries. My detective work is limited to looking about me furtively. Then, at around 2, I make the completely irrational decision to enter The Swan With Two Necks. It is mercifully empty of anyone I recognise, although I still feel compelled to have a drink.

On this occasion time seems to pass quite quickly, and at 3 I meet Geoff in the Oak.

201

The Mountain

"Christ! What happened to you?" I am reminded of our last meeting.

"Been making some enquiries," I slur.

"Better than helping the police with them, I suppose. We'll have one in here, then we should go. I don't like it when my chorizo and feta quiche have gone cold."

The road to Black Ridge meanders for miles through mixed woods, although the approaching darkness and the time spent making my enquiries mean I am aware of little of my surroundings. On one occasion I need a comfort break, and, as I stagger about in the dusk I am aware of a steep drop in front of my unsteady feet. It is with relief that I regain the safety of Geoff's car.

Shortly after 4 we reach our destination – a detached mock- Tudor mansion with imposing gates and enormous grounds, apparently at the very top of Black Ridge. We ring the doorbell and a corpulent, red-faced man of about sixty in a golf sweater opens the door. The sweater appears to have his initials on it.

"Ah yes, friends of Judy," he harrumphs. "In the conservatory, that's where the teaching fraternity seem to be doing most of their lurking. I'm in the main reception room with some from the Lodge. But charge your glasses, first. Judy! That woman and her incessant prattling! Chunter, chunter – Judy! Some - " - he looks around at us – "guests."

Judy and Eleanor emerge from their chuntering, and Judy's face actually turns white. Eleanor's turns the colour of the pale yellow in the multi-coloured kaftan she has donned for the occasion. Unusually, the latter is the first to speak, but she doesn't get far.

"Well!" she begins in an outraged tone.

"No, Eleanor, no!" her friend cuts her short. "No scene here. Frances must know nothing of this whole tawdry affair. Nothing. We'll keep this civilised. A drink

202

The Mountain

for our guests? Mind you, *you*," she looks at me, then
away quickly, "seem to have had a head-start on the rest of
us."

A retainer proffers a tray of what I am sure is the very
finest Cabernet Sauvignon, along with Sancerre and Entre
Deux Mers which are most probably to die for. Ignoring
the etiquette of such occasions, I reach out for two glasses,
put them on what is probably a Louis XVI dresser and take
another two. We head for the conservatory. Assembled
Chapelton High colleagues are present, and the room falls
silent upon our entry. And this time I can see – everyone
looks at their feet.

"Well I fancy the walnut and avocado salad with king
prawns," I slur to Geoff. Such a dish is not visible
anywhere so my mockery is evident to anyone who can
decipher my words. "Thai or Greek?"

I lose track of the rest of the afternoon. Moments of
lucidity come to me sporadically.   At one point I sidle up
to Judy in what I think is the kitchen. There are others
present.

"When I heard you say to Eleanor 'this tawdry affair'
earlier on, was that our affair? The one you wanted?"

"Nigel!!"

"Only it wasn't really an affair, was it? Tawdry, yes.
But not an affair."

"Nigel, there are people present, in case you hadn't
noticed!"

"What? They know about us! Your precious
Frances and his mafia, on the other hand… Anyway, for it
to be an affair, there has to be feelings on both sides,
shurely-"

And then she does it. She flings a glass of her very
best Cabernet Sauvignon in my face, just like they might in
a film. And precious Frances picks exactly that moment to
enter the kitchen.

The Mountain

He storms up to me, grabs me by the throat, his ruddy face and beady little bloodshot eyes inches away from my face, and says:

"Listen, sunshine. Whatever you've done to upset my lady wife, don't even think about it again, or I'll break every bone in your body!"

"What, all of them? The tibia? The fibula? The humerus? Only I'm not laughing." I have no control of what I'm saying, and don't know why I'm saying it. Eleanor comes in, obviously feeling her friend's pain vicariously.

"It's...OK...Frances. Our friend here has had much too much to drink. I'm sure whatever he said, he didn't mean, he probably won't even remember saying it." She looks at me in disgust. "Pathetic. Don't waste your energy on him."

As the evening wears on I become more drunk, and remember little of it. Suddenly I am in a dark room with Geoff. The others have either left or gone to bed. It feels as if it is nearly the next morning. I need to be sick, so with Geoff's help and a torch I stumble outside. Then I notice the garage door is open. Inside it is Judy's car.

Suddenly something comes back to me. Remove the front wheels...trace the pad wear sensor wiring back from the pad and disconnect it at the wiring connector... withdraw the pad...remove the four pads. I'm not entirely sure what it all means, wasn't even sure the first time round, but as if sleepwalking I move towards the garage. And a while later I stumble back into the house, feeling a bit better.

The next morning only Frances is sitting at the breakfast bar – I remember enough to realise he is not my first choice of morning companions.

The Mountain

"A fine state you were in last night!" he begins. "Pah! You young ones can't hold your drink, that's for sure!"

"Frances if I did anything...about the spilt drink...I'm really sorry..."

"Sorry? Pah! Spilt drink was the least of your problems! Don't suppose you remember what you said to Jude and Ellie before you staggered off to bed? Quite disgusting! Shocked a few people. But also quite funny! Pair of stuck up bitches!"

He seems to have mellowed since what I remember of last night. Then he says:

"Fancy a lift anywhere? I'm off down the hill to get some things from the village market. Got to get some bloody eggs, it would seem. Could drop you off."

"No, I'm...Ok...I came with Geoff."

"Left over an hour ago. Took Jude and Ellie into the village early for some god awful horse-show or something this morning. Gymkhana, started at 9, would you believe? Why they can't get the eggs I don't know. But as my car's in for repair, your friend Geoff had to take them first thing, apparently. Now do you want that lift or not?"

Chapter 22

I'm outside the shop an' I'm alone this time. No mates, no Becky or Tracey. Alone. I walks in like I own the place, goes for the glue and solvents section, just grabs some an' goes. Hardly even run. You see, I don't care no more. What the hell have I got to lose?

I'm out of here. I try to run, but this time my heart's not really in it. Up past the Cross, where I get a view of all them grey roofs, an' it feels good to be above 'em. I love these woods. An' my hills. The soft, peaty bits near Brown Moss, the limestone crags by Fenny Brook. An' the birds.

Still summat don't seem right. I've been on the run since last Sunday when that cow Hartington came round to Charon's an' ruined everything. Slept one night up here, freezing. Didn't really sleep. Been tryin' to crash in shop doorways, behind the leisure centre, even near the caravan park – in fact both Coomb's Moss Park an' The Park, which was dangerous (both) but I don't care. It's cold this time of year an' I'm tired of runnin' an' hidin', but I also don't care. An' what the hell have I got to lose?

I can't see Becky or Tracey – the pigs'll be all over them, followin' them, livin' at their houses for all I know. Anyway they'll be under a lot of pressure to dob me in. It ain't fair. I dunno where Dad is or when I'll see Darren, an' I sure as hell ain't lookin' 'cos again, the pigs'll be watchin' em and followin' 'em an' they'll be tryin' to force 'em to dob me in as well.

The Mountain

After Charon let me down bad an' abandoned me I got no-one left in the world. An' that don't feel good.

So I'm up here on top of the hill, the Cross, the highest point of Chapelton. An' I should feel on top of the world. Yeh *right*. I've got my glue. Lighter fuel. Nail varnish. Some educated smart arse like Charon would probably say 'belt and braces', or some crap like that. Well I wanna make sure. I wanna be sure.

I gets out a plastic bag, no-one'll see me up here an' I don't care anyway. I sniff the glue for as long as I can. Then the other stuff – I got aerosol spray an' what looks like surgical spirit, I just took what I could an' left the shop. I feel the rush immediately, I'm dizzy an' feel like I'm gonna be sick. I'm gonna choke. I think I've taken way too much. So what do I go an' do? I take some more, the same amount as before. It's hittin' my lungs, my blood, it's goin' all around my body. I can actually hear my blood pumpin'. An' even though I don't care about nothing, it's scary.

I can do anything I want to. I can run. I can fly. An' for a little while I run around the Cross. There are some big boulders on the ground, just lyin' about the place. I runs up them an' jumps from the very top. I land on my feet, but only just. I do it again. An' again. An' it feels good, in a sort of freaky way. I get a buzz from it, I'm sweatin' an' cold at the same time. I'm dizzy, I feel I'm choking, an' my face is goin' all numb. My heart is pounding like crazy. An' then comes the mother of all headaches, much earlier than usual, an' much worse.

My temples are poundin', the rain suddenly lashing against my face stings like crazy, the wind nearly knocks me off my feet an' I feel sick. My head is explodin'. This shouldn't happen this early. Maybe I was wrong before, maybe I didn't take enough. Maybe I'm almost addicted to it so I need a bigger dose to get high.

The Mountain

All I'm feelin' now are the bad things, the high only lasted about ten minutes. I'm cheated again, even the scuffin' glue is gangin' up on me. So I reach for the nail varnish an' the plastic bag an' whack it straight up my nose. An' keep it there 'till I feel I wanna pass out.

The buzz I get this time is really strong, I'm well dizzy. Everything is so blurred, I can hardly see. I still feel as though I'm chokin', but the headache's gone, sort of. It just feels numb. My legs an' arms are tinglin', I don't really like the feelin', so I'm shakin' them all over, shakin' the rain off them, shakin' the pins an' needles away. I must look like a wet spastic scarecrow doin' a crazy dance dressed in black. I'm cold again, so I begin to run.

I'm runnin' faster an' faster, higher an' higher', which ain't right 'cos the Cross is the highest point, but the ground goes up an' down, seems to fall away from me then looms up towards me, although I dunno 'cos I can hardly see. An' I'm goin' for ages, faster an' faster, this ain't right, my heart is gonna burst. But I can't stop myself. I'm goin, downhill, too fast, I'm out of control, speedin' out of control, an' I trips on a stone or summat an' rolls an' rolls all the way down the hill.

I stop at an' old bridge. I ache all over, makes a change from bein' numb, although my head is still numb. An' dizzy an' tingling. It's Three Shires Head, I used to come here on a run to listen to the birds. I can hear the lapwing, the snipe thumping around. An' the curlew whirling. It's peaceful, I like it. Except for the river, which is goin' a bit crazy 'cos of all the rain, it's gonna burst. My head is gonna burst. I stand on top of the bridge.

Less than a week ago I was the closest to happy I been in ages. My life was still a mess – pigs, teachers, social workers lookin' for me everywhere, Dad gone, separated from Darren, homeless. But I was nearly happy. Someone cared about me. I was clean, had a flat to stay in

208

The Mountain
(sort of), had food, even nearly dressed up. Since then it's
been a week of hell, it's not the cold or the rain, it's not the
pigs lookin' for me, it's the feeling that nobody cares.
That's harsh on my two real mates, Becky an' Tracey, but
they can't see me. I'm no good to them, I'm trouble,
they're better off without me. Charon don't care, he was a
fake, if he'd cared he wouldn't have left me all afternoon
an' come back with that cow Hartington. She dobbed him
an' me in. But he might have dobbed me in anyway. I'll
never know. If he wasn't gonna dob me in, why did he
come back with her?
       Nothin' makes sense. Separated from Darren
don't make sense. Dad gone don't make sense. Eddie
gone, Mum gone… None of this makes no sense an' I don't
care.

       Then, suddenly, I wake up an' I do care. An' I'm
well scared. I hate myself, I'm useless. I've lost
everything, everyone who ever cared about me. An' I'm
tired. I'm tired of runnin'. I don't wanna be here no more.
But at the same time, I don't care if I live or if I die. Don't
make sense.
       I'm standin' on the bridge, lookin' down at the
water about twenty feet below. It's deep. It's goin'
mental. An' I'm swayin', I'm dizzy, the wind is howlin'
round me an' the rain batterin' my soggy clothes. An' I
dunno what happens, I sway, I wobble, somethin' – the
wind, my mind, the birds, I dunno – somethin' takes me off
my feet an' I fall, fall, fall into the white water below me.
A light goes out inside my head.

       "Anna, you well scared us!" A light is on inside
my head, a light is lookin' into my head. I dunno where I
am.

209

The Mountain

I'm fuzzy all over, have a stinkin' headache, I'm numb yet tingly at the same time. An' I dunno where I am.

It's Tracey's voice, I can just about figure out. Then another voice.

"What was you playin' at? You could have drowned! You was high! You fell in the river at Three Shires Head! You must have run for miles."

It's Becky. This still don't make no sense, but I can recognise voices, though everything's a blur. I dunno where I am. I can't feel nothin' in my whole body, all I can see is this bright light in my face.

I dunno how long I'm like this. For a while, no-one talks. Then I hear random noises, sort of layers of noise on top of each other but changin' position, so the one at the top becomes the one at the bottom, sort of like shufflin' cards. My head hurts. Then a light goes out again.

A lot of noise, some different lights. Then I opens my eyes. A geezer in a white coat is standing over me. An' I'm in a bed, with white sheets. Lights are still shinin' everywhere. I can't really see owt yet, just these lights, I can't hear too clear, then I think the geezer speaks, he goes:

"Well, you certainly gave us all a scare, young lady. Not to mention your friends. It was touch and go, I can tell you. You have been slipping in and out of conscientiousness for the last 48 hours. Touch and go. Full name and date of birth?"

There is a pause. Then I hears Tracey, or is it Becky, she goes:

"She don't talk."

The geezer in the white coat kind of snorts. Then he speaks again.

"Considerable amount of solvents found in your bloodstream. Enough to stun an elephant. Probable

210

respiratory impairment due to submersion in water, considerable water inhalation. What on earth were you doing in such a dangerous environment? If those anglers hadn't seen you washed up on the rocks by the river Dane and alerted a passing horse-rider who called the police – well, it doesn't bear thinking about. We've been in touch with your school. Next of kin?"

This time it is Becky.

"She don't talk. It's not what she does."

The white-coated geezer mutters something to another white coat. Then he turns to me, at least I think he does. He's like:

"A discharge is problematic without the next of kin. Perhaps I can rely on the cooperation of your two friends to help identify a responsible adult who could fulfil that role. We need to notify the police, possibly social workers. For the time being, I recommend some rest. We'll worry about a discharge at a later date. And you, young lady," he peers over my bed, "can think yourself very lucky indeed to be still alive."

The white coats leave the room. I still can't hardly see. I still can't make no sense of owt. I feel safe with Becky an' Tracey.

It's quiet for a long time. I need to rest. It's goin' dark around me again, but this time I think it's OK, 'cos it must be evening. I like feelin' safe.

Becky stands over me an' looks at me. She rests her hand on my forehead. She's like:

"We was worried, you know. Hadn't seen you in a week. School was goin' mental, Osborne, pigs, round at us houses the whole time. We didn't say owt, 'cos we couldn't."

Then Tracey. She goes:

"You got lucky. The horse-rider who went for the ambulance thought you might be a pupil at school. She

211

contacted the school. They came down to the hospital.
Cops interviewed us again, told us you was in here. You
been here two days!"

I can't talk. It's not that I don't, but I can't. I
wanna cry but I can't. Tracey's like:

"We've seen Osborne. We told him an' Darren
that you've been found. Osborne says as far as he's
concerned, you can go back there." She pauses.

"Still no sign of your dad. But it were OK in
there, weren't it?"

I still can't talk. I still wanna cry. Then Becky
goes:

"There's a new band you'd like. I've just noticed
them. I brought a cassette. When you get out of here, we
can have a proper listen."

Becky approaches the bed an' holds my hand.
"They're called The Wedding Present. The songs all sound
the same. Guitarist sounds like he's playin' a banjo.
Singer's proper mardy at times. But he's fit. Fitter than
Morrissey."

Fitter than Morrissey. I looks round, Becky an'
Tracey are still there. I see four big brown, trustin' eyes. I
feel a bit safer now. I'm getting a bit warmer, an' it's quite
OK to be in a bed. The light is still shinin' in me eyes, my
body is still numb, my head aches, an' I still can't talk or
cry. Fitter than Morrissey. Just for now, I'll take that.

2629163R00113

Printed in Great Britain
by Amazon.co.uk, Ltd.,
Marston Gate.